THE CHICAGO SPIRIT CAFE

JH Tomen

ISBN:
ISBN-13: 979-8-9862909-9-7

For Audrey,

There's nothing more inspiring than a soul once freed
turning back to free another.

I promise someday I'll be talented enough to write a spicy fae
book you'll actually enjoy ;)

Cover by Karl Nilsson (@sigvardnilsson)
Spirit drawings by Matt Dye (@mattdyedraws)
Map by Eric Kessler (@internal_combustion_art)
Edits by Joe Pierson

Chapter One

Arnold started seeing spirits. It happened suddenly in college, when he was supposed to be too old to believe in that kind of thing. His grandmother had always talked about "sprites" around the house — little creatures she swore were moving her things — but he'd thought she was just being eccentric. After all, she'd been the one who'd forced his parents to name him Arnold. But here he was, in a bagel shop, staring at a blob on the ceiling. A blob that was looking back at him.

He rubbed his eyes — something his Ma, who worked as an optometrist's assistant, said to never do — as he moved closer. It was behind the counter, in the corner above the toaster. But even stepping toward it, its shape seemed no clearer. *Blob* was still the only word for it, a brown mass with eyes. Thankfully, he had already ordered, so the girl behind the counter didn't notice him as she moved on to the next customer.

Please don't let that be real, he prayed.

Even if it meant his grip on reality was slipping again — normally his greatest fear — it was better than *spirits* being real, right? He pulled out his phone, hoping he could will it away, when it spoke.

Hello, it said. There was no sound to it, no voice in the air, but he could hear it in his mind all the same. He looked back up, the blob's eyes narrowing.

You see me, don't you? I was worried for a second when you pulled out your phone.

Arnold spared a glance for the girl behind the counter, but she was busy explaining what lox was. He looked back at the blob, nodding carefully.

Oh, great, the blob said. *I thought so. You had the look about you — not that there's been many of you lately. Humans have such underdeveloped third eyes these days. It's been…gosh, a decade since someone noticed me. Though the last time didn't exactly end well…*

Arnold opened his mouth, about to speak, when he stopped himself. No one was looking at him now, but they certainly would if he started talking to the ceiling. But how was he meant to speak to a blob? Could his words appear in its mind in the same way? Could he—

Are you real? he thought at the blob. A crinkle appeared in the blob's eyes, a smile appearing out of nowhere.

I assure you I'm most real, the blob said. *I take it by your question you don't speak to spirits often?*

Arnold shook his head.

Everyone's a little different, but from what I understand, it takes time to see us. Sneaks up on you, really. Take Julie. The blob glanced at the direction of the girl behind the counter. *She's in high school, so the owner doesn't take her seriously, but she's said she feels something in the shop. Still, she's never looked directly at me. What's your name?*

Arnold thought his name, leaving off his surname. Did spirits need to know that kind of thing? What if it figured out how to follow him home?

Arnold, the blob repeated as if tasting it. *A good name, an old name. I usually go by Cerno's Bagels with other spirits, since this is where the core of my essence is. But you can call me Poppyseed if you like; those are my favorite.*

Arnold raised an eyebrow despite himself, the blob chuckling in his mind.

I take it you thought I was a person? Not many spirits are, actually. Sometimes a ghost gets stuck or something, but even passing on, you humans are always in a hurry. No one's died in the bagel shop in a while, though I've seen others in the neighborhood. You're like little flames, lights rising into the sky like smoke. It seems peaceful.

What…are you, then? Arnold asked, his mouth feeling dry even if he didn't need to talk.

You know how they boil bagels? "Boil then bake or end up with cake?" Well, right before they boil, they punch a hole in the bagel. And me? I'm the spirit of where the dough used to be.

Arnold frowned, studying the outline of the vague, brown shape. It didn't *look* much like a bagel — or the hole in one's center.

Believe me, I get it. You may not know a lot about making bagels, but it's not like the dough goes anywhere — they're not doughnuts. It just becomes part of the bagel, the dough shaped into a ring. So why is that worthy of a spirit? I could choose to be offended, but I've asked myself the same thing. Honestly, though, I haven't found a good answer. Spirits form where they're meant to, and here I am.

Now, you're probably wondering: Am I just some other kind of spirit attracted to bagels? I mean, bagels weren't invented until the 1600s, after all. But it doesn't seem like it. I've met a few collector spirits — especially the roving kind more likely to stumble into a bagel store — and we look nothing alike.

Besides, collector spirits are solitary creatures, and I'm hardly alone. I can feel all these other bagel stores, these little pieces of me growing toward each other like mushrooms in a forest. There's a limit to my radius — not even a spiritual organism can reach infinity — but it goes for miles. Honestly, I pity the bagel spirits of New York, jammed in together between the piles of toasted everything and—

"Sir?" a voice asked. Arnold blinked, looking down to see the girl holding out his order, a worried look on her face. "Your order?"

"Oh, thanks," he said, taking the bag. Maybe he really was losing his mind, listening to the spirit of bagel holes. But at least he'd come back to reality; at least he was holding his order in his hand. It was warm, and real, and—

Where was I? the blob asked in his head. Arnold looked up, realizing the spirit hadn't vanished. But the bagel in his hand… He looked between the two, feeling a tingle in his spine. So, this *was* real? He was holding his bagel, *and* there was a spirit in his head? He hadn't blacked out or lost the thread in his reality. So, that meant…

He looked at the register, the girl frowning in his direction before turning to the next customer. *Act normal.* He hurried to a table in the corner, pulling his bagel out of the bag. He could pretend to be eating, spacing out with a bagel in hand, right?

Don't worry about her, the blob said, meeting his eyes again. *We get all sorts of strange customers in here, and believe me, you're hardly the strangest. She won't call the authorities on you or anything.*

How reassuring, Arnold thought back. *I guess…you're real, then?*

You ask that after I've spent five minutes explaining myself? The blob sounded indignant — not that it stopped his diatribe for long. *Well, if you're going to stay to have your bagel, I hope you'll indulge me a little further. There's just so much I want to say! I'm always stuck listening, absorbing the world.*

Anyway, I think being a bagel spirit is about longing. A hole, after all, is just an empty space. But holes have potential — limitless potential, if you think about it. I see you looking at your bagel, thinking "this doesn't look limitless to me," but it is! The space between two molecules can be compressed into nothing, a curved line that never reaches the plane, a—

Arnold took a bite of his bagel, hardly tasting it as he stared into the table. At least it was warm, grounding him as the spirit droned on in his mind. How did it know all this stuff, anyway? It sounded more like his philosophy professor than a bagel. Did Poppyseed really— He froze, about to take another bite. Was he really calling it by name, treating it like reality?

You stopped listening, didn't you?

Arnold looked up, shaking his head — though the now-free girl from the register noticed, giving him what had to be her hundredth dirty look. He looked back down, forcing himself to take another bite.

Sorry, he thought to Poppyseed. *It's just…a lot. And I'm gonna be late for class.*

Don't you want to know if I have any requests?

Requests? Like…unfinished business?

Not exactly, the spirit thought, chuckling. *I told you, I'm not a person! Still, I've seen other spirits freed by fulfilling a request. They disappear just like humans, floating into the sky — except they explode like fireworks. It's sort of beautiful, really. I hadn't really thought about it before, but now that you're here… I feel a need bubbling up inside of me, something I've never told anyone. I want to go to a cafe.*

A…cafe? Arnold asked. *Aren't you in one now? I mean, you guys sell coffee and everything.*

Not a human cafe, Poppyseed said, sighing even though he didn't seem to have lungs. *A cafe for spirits. I've realized talking to you that I miss — well, talking. I want to go somewhere with other spirits, somewhere I can make friends. I think if I do that, I'll be free. Another spirit will probably form here eventually — it might even be me again, simply reformed from the same essence — but I want it all the same. Would you do that for me?*

Arnold's bagel was done, his excuse for lingering in the shop gone. He had to be at class in a few minutes, and Northeastern's campus was across the river from the bagel shop. Still, he stayed. It was absurd, terrifying even, but part of him felt…*electric* too. They were reading *The Magic Mountain* in his lit class, and he felt like Castorp in a way, longing to leave behind the flatlands of his boring life. Even if admitting his life was boring felt like a sacrilege. It wasn't long ago that he'd nearly lost everything…

He stopped for a moment, taking a breath. Maybe seeing spirits would derail all his plans, maybe it would only get him in trouble, but what was the point of a psychology degree when you could grant wishes? He could actually *do* something for once. Wasn't *that* the point of being alive?

I'll help you, Arnold thought before he could regret it. *But where's there a cafe like that? And how can I get you there?*

The spirit laughed, the sound oddly like shaking a jar of toppings.

Ah, the spirit sighed, finally catching its "breath." *I forgot how funny humans are. There aren't any coffee shops like that. You'll need to build one.*

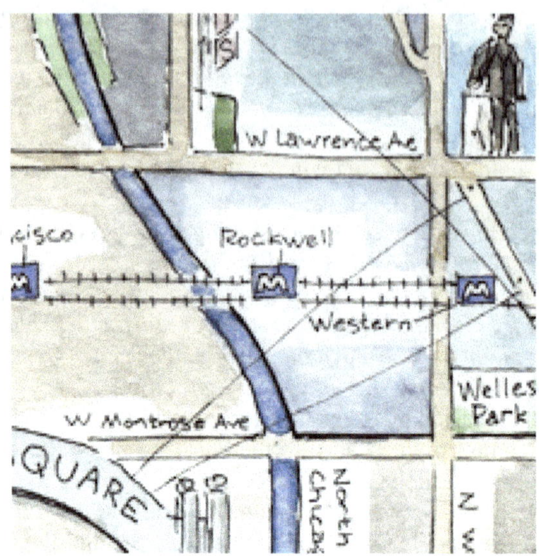

Chapter Two

Helen leaned over the open oven, the heat burning against her face. The muffins she was baking had turned a golden brown on top, but something still seemed off. They should have smelled…happier. *Happier?* Was she really willing to admit that to herself? At least she hadn't said it out loud to anyone yet, but the realization had been lurking on the edges of her mind. For weeks now, she'd been…*baking feelings.*

Helen shut the oven, leaning against the counter as she stared into the floor, trying to summon the flavor again. Like something from a dream, these new ideas simply appeared, flaky crusts drifting through the void. Around them, she could sense their connection to memories, some fragment from her life they wanted to convey. They weren't recipes exactly, but her tongue seemed to know just what they needed. She knew if she could find the right ingredients, the feeling would be there.

At first, each new recipe she'd pictured in her mind had held only a single feeling — which had made the strangeness of it all easier to ignore. After all, brownies were *supposed* to bring you joy, weren't they? Just because cookies helped you through a breakup didn't mean they were magic. Unfortunately, it was quickly becoming more than that. The feelings were…*growing.* Still, with a bit of grit, she might have managed to ignore it forever. But a few weeks earlier, she'd overheard a pair of customers talking, forcing it all to click in her mind. *This was real.*

The women had come in on a Saturday looking for coffee. They were elegant, willowy things, completely out of step with the neighborhood. One of them had worn an orange scarf, while the other had a yellow handbag that looked European.

"Do you serve coffee here?" orange scarf had asked, looking around the shop.

The shop was such a simple place, even if it was everything Helen had ever dreamed of. It had been Gran's once, and she'd inherited the apartment above it too. She'd spent a huge amount of her savings fixing it up — replacing the oven, fixing the display case — but she was finally open, fulfilling both her *and* Gran's dreams. Sure, the fans squeaked, and the hinges on the walk-in were getting rusty, but none of that mattered. It was *hers*.

"We do," Helen said, trying to use her chipper sales voice, though it came out as more of a squeak. She turned to point at the chalkboard hanging up behind her. Was the chalkboard unclear? It said coffee in big, bold letters she'd drawn herself, her roommate getting one of the designers in her office to do a dozen drawings of cats to go with it. Cats sitting in coffee cups, cats playing with bread. Did fancy women hate cats? Would no one buy cat coffee? The espresso machine rental alone was a nightmare. Had she bankrupted herself for nothing?

"Our savior!" yellow purse said, laughing. "The line at the other place was absurd."

There was, in fact, much better coffee down the block. Still, they were more than lacking in the pastry department, and they seemed to send about a dozen customers her way on any given weekend morning, enough that she'd started earning a few not-so-terrible reviews.

"How about a cappuccino?" Helen offered. "There's…uh…mocha muffins to go with them."

She left out the part about the muffins having *determination* baked into them. That was only a silly thing from her imagination anyway, wasn't it? But to her infinite surprise, the women had agreed to both without a second thought, swiping a black card on her tablet before they retreated to a table in the corner.

Helen had brought them their order as quickly as possible, but the women seemed to have ducked inside less to avoid the line — and the early spring chill — and more to gossip. They hardly seemed to notice her at all when she set the coffees down, launching into a heated discussion over what sounded like orange scarf's husband.

"You already know what I think," yellow purse said, pointing with her muffin hand. "You should've left him years ago, after Cancun. Don't tell me this time is nothing too. I've listened to too many tears over the years to keep ignoring it."

"I guess," orange scarf said, staring into her coffee. "It just really seemed like he'd changed."

Part of Helen wanted to take notes — assuming yellow purse was successful — to give herself a glimmer of hope of convincing her roommate, Em, to dump her boyfriend. Helen and Em weren't quite as fancy as these two, but a dirtbag boyfriend was a dirtbag boyfriend. Aside from all the borderline abusive fights Em had with him, her so-called "chef" of a boyfriend made an awful mess in their kitchen at least twice a week — a mess Helen often found herself cleaning up despite her many hours scrubbing pans in the bakery.

Helen pretended to be busy as she eavesdropped, wiping the counter for the hundredth time when everything changed. Something *magnetic* filled the air, drawing her eyes toward the women just as orange scarf took a bite of her muffin. Orange scarf froze, her eyes transfixed as she chewed. As she swallowed, she licked her lips, closing her eyes.

"And?" yellow purse asked, cocking an eyebrow at her.

"And…you're right. It's time. I'm leaving him."

When the women finally left, marching out of the coffee shop like soldiers on parade, Helen had stood by their table for a long time, staring at the abandoned mugs and plates. Could it have been her muffin? Could the determination she'd baked into them — something she thought *might* have come from the way she'd sprinkled in the chocolate chips — have influenced this woman to make a decision she'd been avoiding? Either she really was losing her mind, or it was proof. Proof of something absurd, and foolish, and…*amazing.*

Now, she couldn't seem to escape this new kind of baking. Recipes seemed to fall on her from the sky, crashing into her fully formed as she went about her day, the emotions growing increasingly obscure. Take the muffins she was baking now. This one had come to her while she'd been on the couch the night before. It was *sort of* a happy feeling, but it was more complicated than that. Happiness with a bit of…*defiance* in it.

Em had been arguing with her boyfriend in the other room while Helen drowned out the noise with the TV — and a show about two chicken growers competing with each other for the perfect egg. She was completely comfortable under her blanket, her eyes growing heavy. She wanted to go to bed, but she didn't want to brush her teeth yet, her laziness and comfort at war with each other. She'd been nodding off — lurching awake each time her head rolled off the pillow — when the recipe had come. Like a truck driven straight through her apartment, she'd bolted upright, writing down everything she could before she forgot.

Unfortunately, it wasn't like magic recipes came with clear instructions. It was more of a flavor pushed onto her tastebuds, a sudden jolt of *knowing*, of feeling like her new bake was something she could reach out and touch. This one, though — *bed resistance*, she was calling it — was tricky. She'd known straight away the muffins would have turmeric in them, which gave them the golden color. But after three attempts, something was still missing. At this rate, she'd lose the bakery to flour costs alone — her usual, emotion-free fudge brownies barely keeping the lights on.

But she had reason to hope, didn't she? A week after those women had visited, a review had come in, putting her on a course she refused to take herself off of. It had been short, achingly so, but the profile picture had looked just like orange scarf, her five words and five tiny stars altering the bakery forever: *This muffin changed my life.*

Helen might be risking everything chasing these feelings. Who even wanted a baked good that made you feel like you didn't want to go to bed? But something told her to push forward. If she could only figure out how to make this feeling, she could find others, feelings to help her customers, her neighborhood, her city. And deep down, she knew she also had to help herself. If she couldn't shake this ache, this…*melancholy* she'd been clinging to these past few months, she wasn't sure how long she'd be able to keep the bakery going anyway.

"Lemon," she said, shutting the oven door. "It's lemon!"

She ran into the kitchen, her workstation hidden from the cafe by the counter. Maybe lemon frosting on a turmeric cupcake was absurd, but at the moment, it tasted just like hope.

Chapter Three

Nüste sat by the window, sighing as the people passed below. It was raining, which should have been a good thing — water from the sky, new plants shooting up, *life* — but it wasn't. Winter was still holding on as spring barged in, the water doing little more than wetting the salty slush already on the street. And it made the attic damp, scaring away the fragments of dust spirits who sometimes appeared in the boxes of antiques, the only companions he ever seemed to find these days.

He? Some spirits had genders, though his kind normally didn't. He was a spirit of new beginnings, and he was meant to be free, to float through the prisms of being, like dandelion fluff. He was shaped like a little mushroom with legs, his form designed to quite literally *sprout* from the source of a beginning. But already, he could feel himself growing more corporeal, attaching himself to the attic. Just another risk of lingering too long in the human realm, it seemed. He should have moved on by now, but instead, he was *stuck*.

So, Nüste sighed again, even if it did little to relieve his gloom. Humans sighed all the time, though, didn't they? It must have *some* effect. But if that were the case, then why did the humans seem to resist helping themselves so much? They walked by at a steady pace, a stream of humanity heading for the train, the Brown Line rushing by every seven minutes as it shuttled them to their offices.

He used to think humans loved change. When he was younger, seven hundred years ago, he'd thought change was all they did. But all the humans he saw now seemed stuck. Maybe they wanted things to be different — they certainly talked like they did — but they never seemed to *do* anything about it. They just put their heads down, trudging to the train, there and back, there and back. But didn't they long for more? Spirits always *wanted* something, appearing around the energies that formed them. And humans had spirits hiding in those fleshy bodies. Unless they were spirits who fed on drudgery…

Nüste heard footsteps below, and he turned toward the door, hoping the home's owner might come into the attic. But she never did. The footsteps faded away, silence settling into the house again. There was something he was missing here — something they were *both* missing — and until he solved it, he probably wouldn't move on. And neither would Helen…

He'd appeared in the attic the day she moved in. It was still chaotic then — movers, friends, music. At first, he'd thought he might have been brought here by the move. But then, why stuff him in the attic? Then, he'd started hearing about the bakery she was running on the ground floor. That was certainly a new beginning, but if so, why hadn't he vanished as soon as the bakery opened?

Helen complained sometimes — to her roommate, whenever the other girl wasn't fighting with her boyfriend — about how things were going. The cost of flour, the rats out back, the customers. Was that it? He'd never bonded to a business before. Like a seagull perched upon a ship, maybe he couldn't leave until they'd safely cleared the harbor.

Or maybe it was the *feelings* the girl kept looking for. There was a…darkness to the attic, an energy lodged between the boxes. He couldn't look at it directly, not yet, but he could feel it. It pulled at him, exerting a sort of gravity over his essence. But it wasn't the only thing he felt. He could sense a flood of feelings from below, *pure emotions* somehow released by Helen. He could see one in the bakery now, in his mind's eye, a swirl of color.

Emotions were everywhere, of course — they were the third leg of the spirit realm. Usually, though, they were muddled things, slipping in and out of human consciousness like oxygen in their lungs. When emotions were pure, however, they were almost spirits in their own right, the very idea of them so crystalized as to nearly become embodied. But the emotions Helen kept generating were *strange,* far beyond what he'd ever seen a human knowingly interact with. Even stranger, there seemed to be a new one every day, exploding with color and light before it slipped out through the windows, drifting into the sky, where it broke apart like clouds.

Whatever Helen's new beginning was, she hadn't found it yet. But if it had to do with pure emotions, then maybe he could help. After all, if it was of the spirit realm, it would mean Helen — so regrettably human — would be hopeless at it. Nüste may be trapped in an attic. He may be bound to a dusty, mildewed place with no hope of advancement. But he *knew* emotions. He would find someone to help. He would generate the emotion Helen needed, and then, he would free himself.

Chapter Four

The Brown Line rumbled east, taking Arnold with it, the city rising up around him like a cicada emerging from the ground. Up at NEIU, it was like being on another planet, the school tucked away between a cemetery and a forest preserve, the usual landmarks scrubbed away by greenery. It was beautiful, but jarring, in a way. Now, he felt like he was in a Makoto Shinkai movie, the train slipping along at ground level, a thousand magical possibilities blooming all around him — even if he'd had his fill of magic lately.

He was grateful for the solo seats on the Brown Line — one of the only lines that offered them — allowing him to tuck himself away. Normally, he liked seeing all the people on the train, regarding the silent windows into their lives. But today, he wanted to disappear. It had been a week since he saw the bagel spirit — bagel *hole* spirit? spirit of the void between bagels? — and already it felt like it was draining the life out of him. At first, he'd been excited, true, but that had been *one* spirit in *one* location. Now they were popping up everywhere, and he was beginning to tiptoe through his own life, terrified of what he might find — or *invent* — as he became less certain of his grip on reality.

Still, frightening as it was, this didn't *feel* like last time, when he'd gotten in all that trouble out east. This time, his life had kept going on around him. He'd even enjoyed class for once, allowing him to forget that he was years older than his classmates. Maybe it wasn't his original plan, but after what Ma kept euphemistically calling "the incident," he was grateful to have a life at all. The only problem was reckoning with this…*thing* that wouldn't go away.

He hadn't gone back to Cerno's Bagels. He felt bad about it, abandoning the bagel hole like that after the creature — spirit, *thing?* — had spent decades without a friend. Even worse, he hadn't fulfilled his promise. Even if he had no idea what a spirit cafe was, he certainly wasn't going about building one as he'd said he would.

And yet, it wasn't like avoiding the bagel shop had helped him much. Every time he passed Bohemian Cemetery now, the place was full of lights, the spirits of people drifting into the sky, just like Poppyseed had said. School had been blessedly safe — perhaps with the exception of the library, which he'd ducked out of after seeing something hanging around the books — but few other places were. There seemed to be spirits everywhere, shapes and colors he couldn't explain, trailing him around the city.

Even today, boarding the Brown Line at Kedzie, he was sure he saw something shaped like a turtle on the roof. Thankfully, it hadn't looked at him, pointing itself in the direction the train was about to go. He'd ducked into the train car as quickly as he could, leading him to where he was now, hunched over in his seat, hiding from the world. He had his phone out, but he wasn't really looking at it. He could *feel* the turtle thing above him. If only it were warm enough to bike! School was too far to walk, and his job didn't pay nearly enough for him to be taking cabs.

But he hadn't seen the turtle on his way to school, had he? It didn't help that he didn't know what kind of spirit it was. Maybe it was only attracted to afternoons, a certain feeling the passengers had when they were done for the day, when they— Was he really taking this seriously? He took a deep breath, trying to steady himself — though it earned him a look from the old babushka sitting across from him. Maybe he just needed some food. After all, without the bagel place, he barely had breakfast at all — a recipe for disaster between his pills and the coffee he kept chugging at the Student Union.

"Now approaching Rockwell," the intercom said overhead, announcing the next station. *Rockwell…* His cousin had posted something there the week before, some new bakery. That could be exactly what he needed! A *new* bakery wouldn't even have time to collect spirits, right? It would be strange to start a new tradition after years of bagels, but it had to be better than starving — or facing Poppyseed again.

He waited until the last second to jump through the doors, landing on the old wooden platform just as the train began to pull away. He glanced at the turtle, the giant thing swiveling an ancient yellow eye toward him. Everything seemed to freeze as they looked at each other, the turtle's eye widening.

Young man! it called out, its voice like an ancient boulder cracking. But the train was pulling away. *Young man!* Arnold raised a hand in apology, ducking his head as he hurried for the exit.

He found the cafe on the same block as the station. It was a beautiful building — and one he thought he remembered being abandoned the year before — with old polished wood on the walls and green terracotta on the awning. There was an apartment above it and a sign in the window with a cute little cat drawn on it. In fact, everything about the place was cuter than the pictures he'd seen online. Maybe it was the weather, but the inside seemed to pop, the pink chairs and warm light calling to him.

He ducked in out of the cold but stopped in the doorway, finding one of the most stunning women he'd ever seen. She had her head in the bakery case, arranging a row of cupcakes. But even under the shimmer of the glass, she was like no one he'd ever seen. She looked up as the bell chimed above the door, smiling as she started to talk, though her words were muffled by the glass. She looked around her as if she'd forgotten, crawling out as she wiped her hands on her apron.

"Welcome!" she said. "And…sorry about that."

She had a round face with dimples that looked like they'd been painted on by her perfect smile. Her hair was back, but her bangs still framed her forehead. Somehow, she was more perfect than the cupcakes she'd just lined up, everything about her seeming like an ode to sweetness. Arnold smiled himself, mirroring her before he knew what he was doing.

"Hey," he said, his voice sounding strange as he came up to the counter. "It's…uh…no problem."

He hadn't really thought about women lately. Both his parents were constantly pestering him to get on a dating app, saying it'd be "good for him" to have a girlfriend — as if his calendar were the only issue. Ignoring the fact that he was in no state to subject a woman to his problems, they seemed to think love would fix him somehow.

"What can I get you?" the woman asked.

He flicked his eyes over the menu, though it seemed like hieroglyphics with the way his head was spinning.

"What's good? I was just trying to get something to eat after school."

"Oh yeah? Where do you go to school?"

"NEIU?" he asked, though it wasn't a question. "I'm, uh…studying psychology."

"Cool," she said, still smiling like it was the easiest thing in the world to do. His own smile was already starting to hurt his cheeks, the gesture too foreign for his muscles to adapt to. "Well, these cupcakes are just out of the oven — lemon turmeric. But you might want to avoid them if you have a busy day; might make you lazy."

"The cupcake? Can it…do that?"

"Oh…uh…sugar crash?" she said quickly, chuckling. "They're not…*magic* or anything."

"Uh…sure. Maybe I should get a coffee, though — for the laziness? I do have homework."

"Ugh, homework," she said, sticking out her tongue at the mere taste of the word. "I don't miss that. Not that I don't wish I'd studied harder."

"Have you been baking long? My cousin said this place is new."

"*Very* new! You'll have to thank your cousin for me. We just opened a couple months ago, though I'm not new to baking. I started with my Gran when I was five. She used to live above this place."

"Wow," Arnold said, looking up as if he could see the apartment through the ceiling. "Congrats."

They seemed like they were similar in age, though she was a *real* adult, whereas his failure to launch felt like it had taken a decade off his life experience. He felt the familiar spike of shame crawling up his neck, but at least that was better than staring at this beautiful woman like a kid outside a fish tank. He should get his cupcake and go before he wasted any more of her time. He'd take his food to go and start the walk home. That way he——

She reached into the cooler, putting his cupcake on a plate, and he couldn't find the will to stop her. At least he was a fast eater, right? After all, what was five more minutes? It wasn't like there were any other customers this time of day.

He ordered the first coffee his eyes landed on, though he hardly knew anything about espresso. It was called a "Coffee Cat," but the board said it had nutmeg and cinnamon in it, so he couldn't have gone that wrong. More importantly, the woman's eyes lit up, making him want to order one every day for the rest of his life.

"You're my first Coffee Cat. I was starting to worry no one would ever order it!"

She handed him his cupcake, urging him to go find a seat while she made the coffee. There were only a handful of tables, so he took the one nearest the door, looking out the window — and studiously avoiding looking at the woman as milk hissed on the espresso machine. *Get it together*, he thought, part of him wondering if he wouldn't have been better off risking the bagel store again.

She finally emerged from behind the counter, carrying a giant pink mug in both hands. On top, drawn in the whites and browns of steamed milk, was a tiny brown cat, its tongue sticking out.

"Tada!" she said, setting down his coffee before sitting across from him. She seemed to have done it by accident, though, popping out of the chair a second later.

"Sorry," she said, laughing. Had he been alone too long, or did all women have such perfect laughs? "I'm a little nervous. I haven't made those cupcakes before. Gotta stick around to make sure they aren't poisonous, you know?"

"They could be poisonous?"

"Sorry, no. I mean…*bad*. Goodness! Poison in a bakery? It's like saying *bomb* in an airport!"

"Well, you're welcome to sit," Arnold said, laughing himself. "It *is* your bakery, after all."

She looked at the door, though there wasn't really anyone on the street this time of day.

"Okay," she said, sitting. "As long as you don't mind."

"Not at all, though now I'm afraid I'm gonna eat it wrong…"

"I won't look," she said, turning her head, though she swiveled her eyes back toward him, laughing.

"Alright," he said, picking up the cupcake. He'd never thought so hard in his life about how to eat dessert. While it might seem unhinged, he decided to tear it in half. At least that way, he could avoid shoving his face into the frosting. It felt like ripping a cloud, the golden fluff coming apart perfectly. He turned it on its side, all too aware of the cute little lemon drawn on top as he took a bite.

Leaves. He saw them in his mind as clear as day. A memory? He was a kid, at Legion Park with his mom. He could hear the river running somewhere behind him, Ma's voice calling him to the car. It was fall, and they were going out for cocoa, but he didn't want to leave. He'd worked hard kicking all those leaves, and he was lying in the pile, looking at the sky.

He blinked, staring down at the cupcake in his hand, the image gone from his mind. He looked up, the woman's eyes wide as she waited, her lips parted.

"And?" she asked, her hands gripping the edge of the aluminum table.

"Uh…amazing," he said, rubbing the frosting from his mouth he hadn't managed to avoid. But it *was* amazing, incredible even. He hadn't thought of that day in years, though what lying in a pile of leaves had to do with cupcakes was beyond him. Even though it might be the greatest thing he'd ever eaten, he set it down, afraid his next bite would make him look even more bananas.

"Good," she said, standing. "I'll leave you to it. Don't want my reviews to say I'm stalking my customers."

"Not at all," he said quickly, standing himself for some reason. "I…honestly don't know how I'll ever live without them."

She laughed, the sound like a bell ringing in his heart.

"Well then, I guess I'll be seeing more of you."

"I hope so," he said. "I'm Arnold."

"Helen," she said, heading to the back, her smile still seared into his mind.

Chapter Five

When Arnold left the bakery, he felt lighter somehow. Maybe it was the heady combination of caffeine and sugar — or other things not worth mentioning — but he wasn't worried about spirits anymore. And Helen was right, he *did* feel lazy. He didn't even want to think about his homework. He wanted…something totally different, a break from his routine. But what would he do with this newfound freedom? Should he go to Gene's for a sausage? Take the Western bus to Logan Hardware for some pinball? Suddenly, anything felt possible, like he—

Hey! a voice called somewhere above him. His heart sank, knowing his ears hadn't heard anything, the nerve endings prickling in a false way. He wanted to run, to hide, but part of him knew he had nowhere left to go. Spirits really were everywhere. As the illusion of that perfect woman and her lovely little cafe shattered, he felt his hope go with it.

Arnold turned, looking up at the building behind him. On the third floor, where the roof peaked, there was a window. And in it, a tiny little mushroom was jumping up and down. A…*mushroom*? It was looking at him — *through* him, really — its mushroom cap flailing around as it sprang above the windowsill.

Hey, you! Yeah! You can see me, can't you?! I need your help!

"No, no, no," Arnold said, waving up at the attic. He looked around him, suddenly realizing he'd spoken out loud. He glanced through the window of the bakery, but thankfully, Helen was in the back. He stepped to the side, out of sight as he figured out how to speak in his mind again. *I'm sorry, but I can't do anything like that right now. I have somewhere to be.*

You most certainly do not, the mushroom thought, squaring up as if it had its hands on its hips — despite not having anything even remotely resembling hands...or hips. *I can see a pure feeling on you. You got it from the bakery, didn't you? You might have responsibilities, but I can tell you don't want to do them.*

How... Arnold started. *How do you know that?*

I'm a spirit; we know things. The name's Nüste. You gonna help me or not?

I...it depends. What do you want?

The little mushroom laughed in his mind. *That's not a no! You see the cafe down there? I need to start one up here, but for spirits.*

A cafe...that was exactly what Poppyseed had asked for. Was every spirit a caffeine hound, or was there something else they wanted from these cafes?

I don't know, Arnold thought. *This whole spirit thing... I feel strange enough already. I don't think—*

It's for the girl, Nüste thought. *She needs your help, and unless my eyes deceive me, you're feeling more than one pure emotion right now. You like her, don't you?*

Helen? He looked through the window of the bakery again. She'd gone over to the oven, the focus on her face somehow serene, even as she reached into the heat. He'd known her all of ten minutes, but she seemed like a good person. She was so *real*, without an ounce of the falseness so endemic to his own life. She was like sunlight, and now that she'd warmed his planet, how could he ever go back to his frozen darkness?

But why would she possibly need *his* help? And what did it have to do with this spirit? His mind whirled, all the feelings he'd been avoiding the past few days rushing back to him. Part of him — the part that had said yes to Poppyseed — wanted to take the leap. The other part of him, the rational part, was crying out, terrified he was ruining his life. But there was something more than himself now. There was *Helen*.

In a moment, the truth settled on him like a weight. Even if it was a terrible idea, even if it meant diving into the ghosts in Helen's attic, he couldn't leave without trying. Besides — and it killed him a little inside to know how selfish this was — if he ran now, he could never come back, never see that beautiful face again.

Alright, Arnold thought, *I'll help. But I can't listen here; what if she sees me through the window?*

The mushroom smiled, the gesture hardly comforting.

Go around the corner to the other window, anywhere I can see you. We'll talk from there.

———

Nüste watched for a moment, making sure the kid was really staying. Then, as quickly as he could, he dashed across the boxes in the attic. Unfortunately, it was slow going, like running uphill. The power anchoring him to this place was so strong, it even limited his mobility in the attic. He looked toward the center of the attic. Was it that darkness holding him here? He'd have to test it, running all around until he found its epicenter. It was a good thing spirits didn't get sore, though he may have died of boredom if this kid hadn't shown up.

For the first time since he'd arrived, his mushroom cap felt lighter, bouncing above him as he hurried over the mountain of stuff. What were the odds of finding a spirit watcher so early into his imprisonment? He'd been starting to worry it would take decades to find his freedom. But if he could leverage this foolish boy's true love somehow, he could be free by Christmas.

He didn't believe in fate — at least not in the way humans did. Spirits simply accepted the energy of the world. There *were* fate spirits — he saw one once — but they were more attracted to coincidence than driven to create it. If this boy was here, he'd been attracted here. Whatever the reason — vibrational quarks, cosmic energy, human brokenness — Nüste refused to miss this chance. He was a spirit of new beginnings, dammit, and he craved action! If it was finally his turn, he'd take everything the universe offered to him.

Alright, he thought to the boy below, finally reaching the southern-facing window. He breathed heavily despite his lack of lungs, leaning against the glass. The boy had found a bench and was sitting on it, looking over his shoulder. *We're gonna need a lot of spirits.*

Wait, wait, Arnold thought. *This is all going a little fast. What did you say your name was? 'New...stay?'*

Nüste! he shouted in his mind. *Not that I'd expect someone like you to say it right. It has seventeen syllables, though I guess your measly human ears are hearing two. Just...say it however you want. And get ready to take notes! I won't have you screwing this up.*

Okay, okay, Arnold said, raising his palms in surrender. He actually got out a notebook. Was that a good sign? A little obedience would help, but the boy looked meeker than a mouse. For a project of this size — and importance — the kid would need initiative; he'd need *pizazz.*

I can't explain everything to you, but you should at least know what you're looking for. Firstly, if a spirit can't talk to you, it probably won't travel well. I'll take almost any spirit, but don't bring any downers over here. Let's see...

He paced around on his moving box, trying to get his thoughts in order. It was actually hard to put things into words. It was such a human concept — and a boring one at that. He knew from a neuroscientist he'd haunted once that humans at least *thought* in vectors, their synapses connecting until a thought took shape, a hundred different points that made a fabric. Thoughts *spoken,* on the other hand, were fragmented and tedious, like a trail of breadcrumbs. Tough talk for someone trapped in an attic. Nüste took a deep breath; he needed to get this right.

I think the girl is looking for feelings. You'll know those when you see them; they pop up out of nowhere. Try to get those first, but I can work with anything. If you bring me spirits of a certain size — spirits that can talk — they'll shed emotions she can use.

I'm not sure what she needs exactly, but she's…stuck somehow. If you free her, you free me, and then I'll be out of your hair, and you'll be good to…I don't know, woo her? You'll probably mess it up, though, so don't get your hopes up. Now, let me explain passive versus active spirits…

He talked on, the kid taking notes as quickly as he could. The sun was about to go down, and the little chiseler would probably try to weasel out of his responsibilities after sunset. Still, it was a start. Nüste could taste his freedom, and he wouldn't let go of it now.

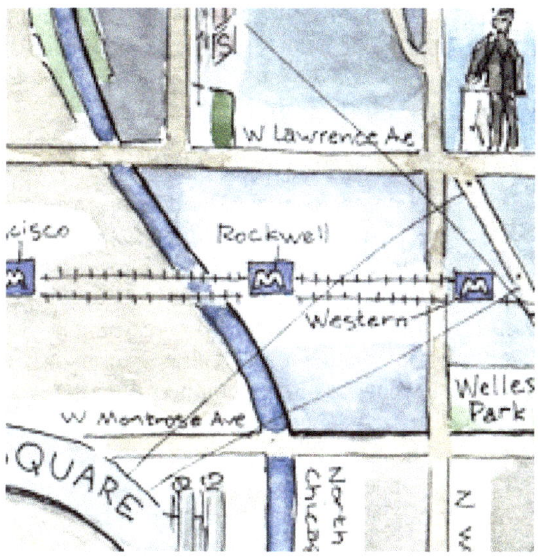

Chapter Six

Helen sat at her kitchen table, her legs tucked up toward her chest, a pile of bills surrounding her. Her math teachers — or frankly, her accountant — would probably tell her it was an undignified position for bookkeeping. Luckily for her, they only said that because they were boring and inflexible — just like these numbers. She needed a hug, and tucking up her legs *almost* made her feel like she was getting one.

She propped her notebook on her knees, doing the math once more. Flour was a major expense, especially since so much of her product still wasn't selling. The food pantry down the street, the Friendship Center, was happy to take her unused baked goods, but she *had* to find a way to stop baking more than she sold. If only she weren't trying to bake her feelings.

Thankfully, Gran had paid off the mortgage on the building before leaving it to her, which kept her from being totally underwater. The place wasn't in the best shape, though, and those costs were slowly mounting. Before moving back to Chicago, she'd had no idea what tuckpointing was, but now she knew all too well. When you built an entire city out of brick in 1890, bad things were bound to happen a century later.

Then there had been the sidewalk crack the city wouldn't fix and the fire extinguishers losing pressure. And all of that was before considering the environmental upgrades she'd made to the place, electrifying what she could to prevent her bakery from spewing carbon into the atmosphere. It hadn't been the greatest couple of months.

But she had a new customer! She had to hold on to that. She'd been thinking about him on and off throughout the day. But why? Because he said he'd come back? Repeat business was the best kind — it wasn't like orange scarf had returned — but…was it more than that? He *was* friendly, and she hardly knew anyone in Chicago anymore. She'd been gone too long, and the people she did know were probably better off staying out of her life.

But she wasn't deluded enough to think friends and customers were the same thing, so what was it? He *was* cute in a dorky kind of way — which was secretly her preference — but being attracted to a customer was even more absurd than thinking they were friends! After the horrendous breakup she'd had leaving Boston, dating again now would be like driving a car without a steering wheel. She wasn't road ready, and if she rushed it, she'd just get them both in a wreck.

I WILL NOT LIKE THIS MAN she wrote in all caps on her notebook. It was hardly double-entry bookkeeping, but maybe her accountant would appreciate some romantic flair. She went back to her numbers after that, though they were of little consolation. The two columns — income and expenses — were hopefully far apart.

Gran had left her some extra money along with the place, though that particular blessing left her feeling strange. Shouldn't Gran have spent it on herself? If not for medical treatment — apparently the cancer was discovered too late — then at least *something.* Skiing? A cruise? Unfortunately, Gran's will had been very clear. She wanted the money to go to Helen, and she'd demanded she open a bakery with it. And Helen had. A strange, nearly broke, delusional, adorable, perfect, dream-come-true little bakery.

She'd just have to write some checks out of Gran's account. But first she'd have to dig up those bank statements. She'd gone to the branch twice, but getting a legacy account online was proving…*interesting.* Still, before she spent even more, she at least ought to know how much was in there — and how much time she had before everything fell apart. The statements were probably in the attic, where the movers had dumped all the extra boxes, her life packed up in a whirlwind after the funeral.

Helen closed her eyes, balling up her fists. She *really* didn't want to go up to the attic. Ignoring the fact that it was creepy — though it certainly had nothing on her God-awful basement — there were too many boxes she wanted to avoid up there, memories threatening to undo all the progress she'd finally made. Even in the kitchen, she could *feel* the attic, the weight of its contents looming up above her. She let her eyes flick over to the attic door. It seemed darker than the rest of the hallway somehow, like a presence — or a fungus — was growing there the longer she avoided it.

There was almost certainly enough money in the account — more money than she'd ever thought she'd have in culinary school. She just wished there was a way to know she wouldn't fail, that her entire life wouldn't prove to be a lie. She'd told herself she'd always wanted this, but now… It felt like someone else's life — or if it *was* hers, then it was one she didn't deserve. She'd always dreamed of having a bakery, baking with Gran in this very kitchen, her hands barely able to reach the counter. But that had been before. Before she'd left, before she tore her family apart.

Maybe that's why she'd started baking feelings, why she was stuck believing in a fairy tale. She couldn't help but hope she might make something special of this place, remaking her dream by doing something good for someone else. She felt helpless, but that's what belief was for, wasn't it? Even the delusional kind. After all, that's why she stayed up every night devouring fantasy novels. Wasn't that the secret hope all people shared? That there was magic in the world? Something they could tap into and unravel all the awful things in life? If only her power was forcing herself to climb up to the attic…

"Nope," she said, throwing down her pencil. "Not today. *Definitely* not today." Tomorrow would be fine, better even. Tomorrow it would be sunnier, the apartment would be brighter, and the attic wouldn't loom over her shoulder like a goddamn ghost.

She leapt from her chair, wandering over to the kitchen. It most certainly wasn't going to solve her bookkeeping problem, but she felt like baking something. She clearly had a problem — compulsive creativity, she'd heard a painter call it once — but baking seemed like the only thing that calmed her anymore. Still, she wasn't an *animal*. She'd bake something savory, allowing her to pretend she was making dinner like a normal person. Everyone needed dinner, right?

All throughout the city, thousands of Chicagoans were doing the very same thing, filling the streets with the smell of supper. Granted, most of them probably hadn't just spent eight hours baking, but that was the sort of quibbling that destroyed dreams. This was her Joan of Arc moment! She was going to bake, and they'd have to bulldoze the building to stop her!

Her triumph, unfortunately, turned out to be a bit short-lived. She spent the next ten minutes banging around the cupboards, searching for something suitable for dinner. It didn't help that Em's boyfriend was a giant man-leech who'd apparently been making his way through her bag of potatoes. Still, between a can of peas, a bit of cream, and a sad-looking carrot, she eventually found enough for a half-decent pot pie.

She cut up the carrot, setting it to sauté with the peas as if they weren't green mush from a can. She secretly liked those better anyway, though she could almost hear the screams of her culinary-school teachers with every bubble in the pan. Making the crust, at least, was like sleepwalking, her hands no longer needing to be told what to do. Her pantry was also choking with baking supplies ready to be used. Even with an industrial kitchen downstairs, there was easily two pounds of butter in the fridge and enough flour to make a snow angel. The first time Em had toured the place, she'd stopped in the doorway, staring at the kitchen.

"Are you in a flour MLM or something?" she'd asked, looking like she might bolt then and there.

Helen rolled out the dough, working quickly so the heat of her hands wouldn't melt the butter. She could go downstairs to roll it out on the stainless steel, but that would defeat the purpose of her rough-and-ready upstairs dinner.

Besides, even if she poured all the love in the world into this dough, it would eventually have to team up with her sad carrots.

The oven let out a sad bleep behind her — the preheating finished — and she started her blind bake. She'd sold her baking beads to a classmate before she moved, but she'd collected a pretty mean jar of pennies for the purpose, shaking them out over parchment paper to weigh down the dough. The vegetables had also cooked down by then, so she poured in the cream.

Hopefully she wasn't clogging her arteries too badly. It was an occupational hazard of running a bakery, though she'd read there was very little evidence to prove high cholesterol wasn't just genetics. Besides, it was Gran who'd made her a butter maniac, and cholesterol wasn't what had brought *her* down.

Helen still hadn't found a doctor since moving back, but that was just one of a million things on every small-business owner's list of "Probably Nevers." There were supposed to be pretty good doctors at Swedish Hospital up the road, but did she really need someone making $500k a year to lecture her about celery? She ran a couple of miles every morning — and hardly *anyone* ran in Chicago, unlike in Boston, where everyone was always desperately sprinting toward Heartbreak Hill.

She also ate exclusively vegetables for lunch, standing like a rabbit in the bakery as she shoveled a salad into her mouth over the sink. But she didn't eat her veggies out of guilt — not when diet culture was just capitalist mind control for women. No, she ate vegetables because they were beautiful, colorful things, the sun incarnate as vitamins and fiber. It took some doing, all that reframing, but once you thought about vegetables as a way to connect with the earth, they went down much easier.

Keys jangled in the door, and Helen looked up, saying her daily prayer that Em would be alone. Maybe it was just being in Gran's house — her roommates in Boston had almost universally had shitty boyfriends — but something about that giant oaf being in her house made her blood boil. Besides, with him treating Em so poorly, it made him a constant topic of conversation, her own personal hell of routinely failed Bechdel tests. She happened to know Em had a very serious job in the Loop — the bakery's easy access to the Brown Line one of its key selling points — but Helen almost never heard about it with all the boyfriend drama.

"Oh, no," Em said, looking at the bubbling cream on the stove, her bags in hand.

"I think you mean 'thank God for yet another perk of living with a baker?'"

"Maybe," Em said, moving to hang her jacket on the coatrack. "But there's also the banging in the morning, and the butter, and the smell."

"The smell? It smells fucking amazing in here!"

"That's the problem. It smells *too* good. It's like living inside a cookie. Do you *want* me to be single?"

Em sat at the counter, pulling out her twin devices. If Helen hadn't known about her job's work phone policy, she would have thought Em was a drug dealer. Maybe every job had its hazards, though she'd take butter-clogged arteries over even *more* screen time.

"I would actually love for you to be single," Helen said, checking on the pie crust.

Em rolled her eyes.

"I feel like I barely found this one, and that was fifteen pounds ago. Don't put me back on the apps, Helen, please. I'm begging you."

Helen put her hands on her hips, holding the kitchen towel like a weapon.

"Anyone would be lucky to have you, you stunning little monster. And if I hear that beer-gut hipster call you Piglet one more time, he's gonna find out how quick a chef's knife can pierce an eyeball."

Em laughed, going back to her phone. Helen never would have thought she could talk like that to a new roommate, but for whatever reason, her boyfriend rage only seemed to make Em like her more. Not everyone in her life had been so charmed by Helen's authenticity, but Em made her feel like maybe she had friends in Chicago after all. It *almost* made her want to blab about her cute new customer — but she knew she couldn't give that line of thinking any oxygen. Besides, she would *not* allow boys to ruin her evening any more than they already had.

"Tell me about work," Helen said, turning back to season the filling. "I need some office drama in my life."

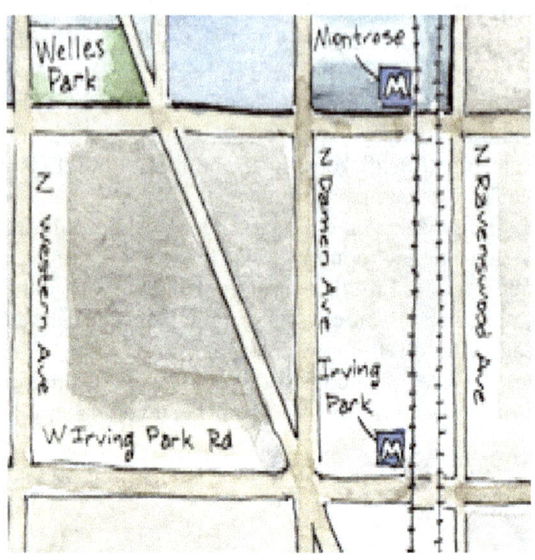

Chapter Seven

Arnold lay in bed the next morning, staring at the ceiling. He traced the water damage with his eyes, like a map that might lead him somewhere. There was a *lot* of water damage. Only partially covered by the "landlord special," the thin coat of white paint did little to hide the kaleidoscopic rings of brown. Was it dangerous? Was there mold? He found he didn't care. The little studio was all he could afford.

He rolled over, reaching for the textbook he'd dropped off the side of the bed. He frowned, rereading the sections he'd highlighted the night before. He had no recollection of reading any of it. His mind had clearly been on other things — like trying to figure out if everything he'd seen the day before was a hallucination. He'd hoped sleeping would clarify things, wash away the parts he'd made up. But there it all was — Nüste, the train, *Helen*. Or had he made her up too?

He sat up, rubbing his face before reaching for his phone. There were two messages waiting for him, though he already knew who they were from.

Take your pills. Love, Ma.

Arnold chuckled. She always signed her texts like they were letters. She also loved the ritual of telling him — every *single* day — to take the pills he'd been dutifully taking for years. Sometimes, her worry made him feel like he was made of glass, that the atoms forming him might pull apart. But how could he be anything but grateful? He'd put Ma through a lot out east, forcing her to drive all the way out to Rhode Island to get him from the hospital.

Maybe she was a little overbearing — and mildly terrifying when she didn't get her way — but that's who she was. She was just…*Ma*. Besides, was she all that wrong about him? He was *seeing things*, and he'd done nothing to stop it. He hadn't rushed to the hospital, hadn't told his doctors. If anything, he'd encouraged it, agreeing to do Nüste's bidding. It wasn't exactly like what had happened out east, true, but could he really trust his own mind anymore?

That was part of the problem, wasn't it? He'd done a lot of reflecting since his life had fallen apart, and he couldn't quite disentangle the parts of him that were whole and the parts that were broken. There was the illness — the breakdown out east, the fears, the whirring in his mind — and there was *him*. The him part *was* different, his OCD making him some form of neurodivergent — something his therapist had helped him realize. It had made so much click, especially when, for him, hard things were easy and easy things were hard.

But embracing that label meant there were parts of his difference that were good, *beautiful* even. The art he used to do, his kindness, the way he categorized information. Those all came from a very real part of him, right? Why couldn't it be *that* part of him that was seeing spirits? Still, Ma wasn't wrong to worry. Besides, by now, Ma's texts were a tradition, something to connect them. It was only her second message that made his stomach drop.

I have a bag for your uncle.

Arnold hated going to Uncle D's. Ma's oldest brother, he was what Dad lovingly described as a "mean son of a bitch." For decades, he'd lived in the woods with a sort of hyper-fundamentalist doomsday cult, only coming back to Chicago when he couldn't take care of himself anymore. Now, Ma had him in a retirement home nearby, and with her late nights at work, Arnold was the family courier.

Look on the bright side, he thought. *Maybe Uncle D knows how to banish spirits or something.* Why join a cult if they didn't teach you exorcism charms? Of course, an old folks' home could also be the perfect place to hunt for Nüste's customers. Either way, for once, he might learn something amidst all the angry preaching and blasting Fox News.

He rolled to a seat, adjusting his sweatshirt from where it had wrapped around him in his sleep. It was from his old school, the big block letters covering most of his chest. He looked down at it, sighing. He kept wearing it hoping it was exposure therapy, but it was also incredibly warm — and he couldn't afford to turn the thermostat up any more than he already had.

He crossed the tiny threshold into the kitchen — a change in flooring only, since his studio had no doors apart from the bathroom. He poured a glass of water, sipping it as he looked out the window. He'd hung up some light catchers, and they rattled as the train rolled past, casting swirling rainbows across the floor. He loved living here. Sure, there was mold, mildew, and the occasional cockroach — he spotted one, smacking it — but it was *his*.

The first year at his parents' house had been harder, leaving him adrift. Now,

he had a job, his own place, a new school. It was good. It was *enough*. It was—
His stomach rumbled. He peeked in the fridge, finding it depressingly bare. When the farmers' market was in season, it felt fun to fill his house with produce. Now, though, with winter just about over, he remembered why he'd been surviving off of bagels and free food in the Student Union.

His phone buzzed, no doubt reminding him it was time to leave for work. He settled on a pile of fortune cookies he'd been hoarding from the occasional takeout from Shanghai Inn. Quickly breaking them into a pile and shoving the fortunes in his pocket — was that good luck or bad? — he shoved the pile into his mouth. Hopefully that would be enough of a base. He took his pills from their place beside the sink, swallowing all of it down with one last gulp of water.

Taken, he texted Ma. *Love you.*

Pulling on his jeans from where he'd left them, he shoved everything into his backpack before stumbling out into the hall. He nearly ran into Lois, his eighty-year-old neighbor from across the hall.

"Well, if it isn't Arnold! How are you, sweetie?" She opened her arms, beckoning him for a hug.

"Good, good," he said, pushing his backpack out of the way so he could lean in without hitting her with his books. "How are you?"

She was a funny woman. She ran a little garden on the building's rooftops — "most definitely *not* landlord-sanctioned" as she said — and he'd helped her carry all sorts of supplies up there the previous summer. He'd never been in her home, but every time she opened the door, he could see dozens of dreamcatchers and other baubles hanging from the ceiling.

Now, though, he found he wanted to visit her place, even if it was just for a cup of tea or something. How did you become more than acquaintances with someone? There always seemed to be a little wall between people, and everyone walked carefully around it, sticking their noses over to say hello. But some people found a way to crack through, didn't they? People...like Helen.

He really did need friends — all the guys he'd grown up with had moved away. In school, he'd always just sort of collected friends, globbing onto the people who could tolerate him. It wasn't so simple as an adult it seemed. You had to be strategic...*winsome,* even. But if he was desperate enough to talk to spirits, then why couldn't Lois be his first *human* friend? After all, she'd taken to hugging him. She probably wouldn't be *mad* if he asked her to do something, right?

"Oh, I'm fine," she said. "Creaky as ever! You going to garden with me this year?"

"Yes!" he blurted out far too quickly. Lois only laughed.

"Eager for vegetables, I see."

"Something like that."

"Well," she said, putting her key in the door, "I'll be up there tomorrow. Be ready to roll up your sleeves!"

Chapter Eight

An hour later, Arnold sat behind the desk at the record shop, sorting through a stack of movies while he nodded along to the music. Since it was a Saturday, the only day he was alone in the shop, he could play whatever he liked. He mostly listened to lo-fi — something that drove the owner crazy. Tony called it "internet music," but he'd also begrudgingly let Arnold add some Chillhop records to the stacks. They actually sold pretty well, which was good news so long as he didn't play them when Tony was in.

Arnold had been hired more for movies anyway, what Tony affectionately called a "personality hire." Or at least it *seemed* affectionate… It was hard to tell with him. Still, he gave Arnold a buyer's stipend, letting him hunt for movies to add to his little corner of the store. When he'd started, they hadn't even had any Kurosawa. Now, they had little sections full of anime, B-horror, and anything else someone might have trouble streaming.

Maybe it wasn't the most useful job in the world, but it was low stakes — especially in Lincoln Square, far from the hipster hordes in Logan who would judge his taste. It *was* a pretty hipstery job, but he didn't think music — or anything, really — was supposed to be exclusionary. Beauty wasn't supposed to make you cool; it was supposed to make you better, *kinder*.

And even if it was the only job he could hold down since he'd moved back home, the longer he did it, the more he liked it. In fact, on a day like this, it seemed vital to his well-being. He didn't have to think about spirits — or school, or Ma, or the thousand other things jumbling around in his head. He could simply stare at a bunch of Miyazaki DVDs, deciding whether or not to organize them by color, or year, or theme, or—

The bell chimed above the door, and Arnold looked up, finding Jimmy stomping in. One of their regulars, he was about Tony's age and ran the dive bar across the street. He couldn't judge with a name like Arnold, but all the old men in the neighborhood were named like kids from *The Sandlot*. It was weird to picture them as children, but they hadn't always been such salty sea dogs, had they?

"The fuck is this?" Jimmy asked, pointing at the record player.

It was actually on one of his favorite tracks, a collab between Loafy Building and Yestalgia. It was hard to describe, but the way the guitar seemed to float above the rest of the music, it felt like being in a bamboo forest, slipping into the sky as your troubles melted away. Or something like that. Arnold's dad had always liked smooth jazz growing up, the dial stuck on Smooth 87.7, his hands strangling the steering after work each day. He'd never understood all that saxophone until he found lo-fi, a place he could bury his own stress. Didn't Jimmy's generation listen to music for the mood?

"Uh…lo-fi?" Arnold said as if it were a question. "You know, beats and stuff?"

"Lo…fi," Jimmy said as if tasting the syllables. He cocked an eyebrow, apparently not liking the flavor. "Tony wouldn't like that. I need more Grateful Dead."

"Under G," Arnold said, pointing, though all Jimmy ever did was go through the same section every week. For a Deadhead, though, he didn't really have a good vibe. He—

As Jimmy walked away, little mountains appeared on his back. They were almost like a hedgehog's spikes, sticking out of his shirt. Except they were *clearly* mountains. Each one had a brown base and a snowy peak, a mix of heights that formed into a range. As they finished forming, a few even had clouds around their bases, floating through the valleys in between.

Arnold blinked, looking away as he stared into the desk, hoping it would disappear. Was that a spirit? Or one of those pure emotions Nüste was talking about? It had appeared suddenly, just like the little spirit had promised they would. But if so, what emotion was that? Condescension? Even if he could harvest it for the cafe, it hardly seemed like a useful feeling.

"I need *Anthem of the Sun!*" Jimmy shouted from the stacks.

"It's not out there?" Arnold asked, standing up, though that only brought those mountains back into view again, forcing him to look away.

"I know how to read, dumbass."

"Alright," Arnold said, walking over to Jimmy without raising his eyes from the floor. "We should have more in the back; can you watch the store?"

"You know where to find me if I steal something."

Great.

Arnold hurried through the *Staff Only* door, poking around the stacks of boxes. Like many of the older buildings in Chicago, in the back, the drywall and drop ceilings simply disappeared, transforming into a sort of open warehouse. It was oddly beautiful, the arched wood from the late 1800s somehow holding up all the brick. There was even an old skylight, the afternoon sun drifting through a haze of dust.

He wandered through a maze of boxes, only partially guided by Tony's loose alphabetization. Luckily, he knew roughly where the Dead records were, feeling more like some explorer wandering the jungle for a certain type of fruit. It was one turn to the left and one turn to the right and then—

Arnold stopped at the end of an aisle, facing a…*thing*. It was massive, like the bagel spirit only…different. Its shape filled the entire wall at the end of the row. It was gray — and not entirely solid — seeming to have hundreds of little clouds swirling through it like dust storms passing over a desert. Was it a spirit? He'd never noticed it before, though this was his first shift since his…*problems* began. Maybe he could get to the box he needed and get out before it noticed him. But that wouldn't help him with Nüste. He needed spirits if he could get them, didn't he?

"Um…excuse me?"

Something shifted in the gray mass, like a current in the air, all the little tornadoes suddenly spinning outward toward the edges of the blob. As they pulled back, the center grew lighter and lighter until a face appeared. The eyes were a strange, soft purple color, and it had…a *mustache*?

"Are you a spirit?" Arnold whispered, suddenly afraid Jimmy would hear him and burst into the back.

The thing let out a strange groan in his mind, like a whale singing underwater. Was that…a yawn? *I am,* it finally said.

And…uh…what kind are you? Arnold asked, forcing himself to keep his mouth shut and think the words.

Dust.

As he listened to the voice, he realized it sounded far away, like an echo coming through a canyon. There had to be millions of dusty places in Chicago. Was this spirit like Poppyseed, attached to multiple locations and attracted to their dusty spots? It might not be *useful* for the Nüste's cafe, exactly, but he could probably get the creature to try an attic. But how to get the spirit there? Nüste had hinted that Arnold could carry them spiritually. But like everything in his instructions, the little mushroom had been vague, chalking up anything Arnold didn't understand to "human foolishness."

I hope this isn't too forward, he thought quickly, almost stammering in his mind — if such a thing was possible — *but would you like to visit a cafe? One for spirits, I mean. It…uh…it's run by another spirit, but it's in an attic, so I'm sure it's dusty there too. You could—*

Noooooooooooooooo, the dust spirit groaned, the cyclones at its edges buzzing with energy.

Oh…uh…sorry, I only thought…

This…place is…an anchor, the spirit thought slowly, each word seeming to come only after a great effort. *No. I…cannot leave.*

The back room *was* extraordinarily dusty. Perhaps the spirit couldn't tolerate just any old dusty place. After all, how many bagels did it take before a bagel spirit appeared? Every coffee shop had a handful of bagels floating around, but it didn't make them a *bagel* shop.

I'm sorry I disturbed you, Arnold said, suddenly feeling bad — even if it was absurd to feel bad for disturbing a dust spirit. Still, he couldn't help but think of the handful of times Tony had him sweep the back. Had that disturbed this creature's lair, ruining his *anchor*? Arnold looked down at his feet, finding a handful of dust bunnies that had caught on the corner of the boxes. As gross as it was to grab a clump of what was essentially hair and dirt, he stooped down, picking one up.

Would you like this? To…make up for my mistake?

The massive creature blinked, even its eyelids made of dust.

Yes.

Arnold took a careful step forward, tossing the dust bunny toward the creature. Somehow, the spirit *grabbed* it, the dust bunny whooshing to join the larger mass.

Well, I'll be going, Arnold thought, leaning forward to root around the Grateful Dead box — miraculously finding the record he needed near the top. *You…uh…have a dusty day now.*

Arnold finally made it back to his desk, having sent a happy Jimmy — or whatever a normal human's approximation of happy was — off with his record. He leaned against the counter, rubbing his forehead. He'd found another spirit, and…it *didn't* want to come to the cafe. How was he meant to feel about that? On the one hand, he still felt terror that the things were everywhere, slowly infesting his normal life. On the other, his impossible task suddenly seemed even harder. Even if spirits were everywhere, what would he do if he couldn't get one to the bakery?

He sighed, picking up one of the DVDs on the desk, staring at the cover absently. It was *Kiki's Delivery Service.* It showed Kiki sitting in her bakery, leaning not unlike he was, glum and surrounded by bread. How would it feel to make something so perfect? Not just a single piece of art, but thousands, the images blending together until they told a story. Arnold had loved animation for as long as he could remember, so much so he'd been studying to be an animator before his incident out east. And now? He was studying psychology, like becoming a herpetologist after being bitten by a snake.

It would be good — presumably — to learn how to help people, people who were struggling just like he had. But animation had always helped him too, hadn't it? Something didn't have to be *real* to change your life. In fact, sometimes that made it easier. He hadn't really thought about it until he'd taken a class on the Philosophy of Art at his old school. They'd been talking about the Impressionists, but it had stuck out to him all the same.

"Abstraction," he remembered the professor saying, "is the heart of art. Otherwise, why bother once photography was invented? What we're doing with art is something very similar to what the human brain has to do anyway. We take a mountain of information and distill it down into something pure.

Simplified, yes, but still true. Look at this Monet. It isn't just an approximation of a lily pad, it's a lily pad's essence. The *heart* of it. The embodiment of an idea, the soul of meaning. If that can't change someone's mind, what will?"

"That's it," Arnold said aloud, looking up. It might not be exactly what Nüste wanted, but what if he just gave one of these movies to Helen? If anyone had ever inspired a pure emotion in him, it was Miyazaki. He wasn't sure what kind of spirit it would make — *awe, beauty, surrealism?* But even if it wasn't the emotion Helen *needed*, it couldn't hurt, right? Although…doing that would mean *talking* to her again.

Part of him had hoped he could do Nüste's work in secret, dropping off his spirits from the street until Helen was saved. She may have said he should come back sometime, but you weren't supposed to *force* your way into being a regular. Regular status was alchemical, some strange combination of logistics and chance, the customer showing up anonymously until it all clicked.

Besides, what would she think if he gave her a movie? He did *not* want her to think he was hitting on her. For one, he didn't want to be creepy. For another, with how beautiful she was, it would only make her think him delusional — even more than he already was for seeing spirits. But what if he was like…*casual* about it? He could drop it off on his way home from work, stopping in for a muffin…

"It'll be fine," he said aloud, the delusion settling on him like armor.

He took a ten from his wallet, paying for the movie before slipping it into his bag. Tony probably wouldn't care if he took it — he knew all too well how cheap he'd bought it wholesale — but it was the principle of the thing. And besides, the better DVD sales were, the more easily Arnold could justify his existence.

He smiled, humming to himself as he went back to work, suddenly feeling like he had a halfway-decent plan. He would give Helen the movie, inspire a pure emotion, and be on his way to saving Nüste. He just had to survive his uncle first.

Chapter Nine

Nüste lay on his back, staring up at the ceiling. After talking to Arnold the day before, he'd spent a few hours pacing around, letting his excitement build. At one point, he'd been feeling so good, a hope spirit had even flown by the window to get a look at him, its blobby pink body floating in the air. Unfortunately, like hope itself, the spirit was fleeting, and it didn't stay to chat — let alone to have a cup of tea. Ultimately, there was nothing for Nüste to do but wait.

Still, looking at the ceiling, things didn't seem quite so bleak anymore. Already, amid the dusty rafters, there were little pools of emotion building, fragments caught on the edges of the house as they floated up from the bakery below. It was a mix of colors, a sort of *spiritual soup* with little bits of joy and anger swirling on the surface. That was one problem solved. He'd figured the emotions would collect — especially with this giant secret hiding in the attic — and it meant he'd actually have something to serve the spirits when they came to his cafe. Otherwise, they'd be forced to feed off of each other, which…could get awkward.

Nüste got up, rolling off the edge of a moving box. It was extremely hard for spirits to move things, but the longer he was stuck here, bonded to the attic, the easier it was getting. He went back to the box he'd started opening. Labeled "china," he'd kicked a hole in the bottom, looking for cups. He'd made sure to make the hole in the box look like a mouse bite, though Helen would have questions if she found her tea set in a circle on the floor. Still, it was a risk worth taking. A cafe needed cups. Besides, she never came up here, and if she did, it would mean he'd succeeded in freeing her, right?

Unfortunately, easier did *not* mean easy. He wiggled through the hole he'd made in the box, climbing up the stacks of plates and bubble wrap to where the tea set sat. Over the last day and a half, he'd managed to move the first cup all of three inches, finally getting it toward the edge of the stack. Now, he put his whole body into it, pushing with his entire essence. The hardest part would be getting it down, but if he could just—

The teacup flipped over the edge, taking Nüste with it. They crashed into the bubble wrap below, Nüste's body just softening the blow enough to keep the cup intact. His body may be incorporeal, but spiritual energy could still wedge between matter — something to do with quarks, though it would take a gravity spirit to explain it properly.

He scrambled up from under the cup, inspecting it for damage. There was a *tiny* crack on one edge, but it would serve well enough for a spirit. Hopefully, Helen didn't care too much about her china. The spiritual energy in the attic was strongest around that *other* box, the one she was avoiding, though that didn't mean the tea set had no emotional value.

He looked toward the door, taking in the only box that truly mattered in the attic. Set inside a maze of others, there was something different about it, an energy that was hard to describe. It was, if not darkness exactly, then something like it. Still, it wasn't a spirit. It had a distinctly human energy, like black holes and broken hearts. It would probably attract a spirit if left unchecked too long, but it was more like a memory, an anchor for a human soul. Helen's soul? If not hers, then at least someone important to her. Nüste's presence could keep this attic safe for a while, but that...*thing*... only raised the stakes of his work here.

Nüste walked toward the box, shuffling across the floor. It seemed to reach for him passively, like a planet's gravitational force. It was actually easier to walk in its direction now, as if the *box* had become the center of the attic. And perhaps it was. He'd known for a while it was his anchor, but if he was able to look at it now, it meant he was becoming more connected to the attic. He wormed his way up the boxes surrounding it, trying to get a closer look. The boxes around it were titled "miscellaneous," though the box full of darkness was anything but.

Nüste reached for it, stretching out his spirit as a human might reach with their hands. And the box...*pushed* him away. An equation entered his mind, a tiny math spirit flowering above his head, its daisy-like shape giggling as it disappeared. It was the equation for infinite growth and decay, $y=ab^x$.

Things like that happened to him all the time. After all, spirits were basically just piles of math themselves — even if he'd never heard of a human discovering their full equations. Still, he'd never seen one so brightly in his mind, its meaning horribly clear. Until he cleared away this energy, he would be forever bound to it, just as he would never get close enough to touch it on his own.

Nüste sat with his back facing the box, closing his eyes. He felt it tug against his form, his bond to the anchor more noticeable when he was completely still. Whatever was in that box, *it* — and not the bakery — was Helen's new beginning; he was sure of it now. Unfortunately, in his thousands of years of life, this was probably his toughest case. An anchor like that wouldn't fade with time. Human emotions were strange, powerful things, and it would grow stronger every day. Even if Helen died or the house burned down, he would be anchored here.

That girl better be careful with her oven, he thought, shaking his head.

He stood, going back to his work. There was no point in being anxious. He was a spirit, and if his job was to stay here for the rest of time, he would have no choice but to get on with it. Perhaps it would even change his nature, turning him into a spirit of forgotten memories or something. As long as he was Nüste, though, he would do everything in his power to get Helen to open that box.

Chapter Ten

Arnold waited for the elevator in his uncle's building, a pink box of macarons in one hand and Ma's grocery bag in the other. The macarons were his own little peace offering, Uncle D's apartment located in the giant building behind the Lycée Français de Chicago. It wasn't likely to help much — his uncle tended to think little of everyone and everything — but he had to try, right? Anything to keep his uncle from criticizing him was another moment he had to plan his escape.

Maybe it was his own failure to launch weighing on him, but there was something about your worst family member that immediately transported you to all the awfulness of childhood. And on Ma's side of the family, basically every aunt and uncle had turned out awfully mean. In fact, it was a wonder Ma had turned out normal at all. Assuming she *was* normal, of course.

His running theory — crafted over decades of tortured Thanksgivings — was that the seventies had ruined them all, some combination of lead paint and tumultuous times. Ma was just a kid then — the youngest of six — but her siblings had all been full-blown hippies. Then, just as suddenly in the eighties, they'd all staged revolts in the opposite direction, each of them becoming far-right fundamentalists in one form or another. One aunt even claimed to be a prophet, telling Ma about her dreams and what her holy instructions for the family were.

Uncle D, though, had probably gone further than any of them. He'd joined a millenarian movement, citing Micah and Revelation as a call to pool all his money with a preacher and buy a bunch of land on a mountain. They'd picked a spot in northern Michigan, seven hours from Chicago, so they could "get away from the corruption of society." Never mind that they all found jobs as postmen or police in their rural county — surviving off the government they were sure was satanist. They just wanted to be gone from everything they knew.

Unfortunately, Arnold had been forced to spend long stretches on that mountain in the summers, something his parents had euphemistically named "cousin's camp." His uncle had built a little cabin where he lived with a few of the others, drinking well water — that wound up being contaminated — and hiking up the mountain with their bibles in the morning.

He would spend weeks sleeping outside in a tent, his city ways apparently too dangerous to let inside. At night, they'd all sit around a fire, making hot dogs — despite them being "kosher lies" according to Uncle D. Arnold had been pudgier then, and the criticism never seemed to stop, down to how much ketchup he put on the single hot dog he *was* allowed to have.

"Do you have any idea how much ketchup costs?" one of the group's leaders had asked one time, snatching the bottle from Arnold's tiny nine-year-old hand.

"Uh…$2.60?" he'd guessed. He still remembered the answer, so oddly specific for a kid who didn't do the shopping yet. Unfortunately, he'd paid the price for his little study in inflation, earning him a night in the woods *without* the tent, the bugs screaming so loud he hadn't fallen asleep until just before dawn.

The elevator finally opened, taking him up to his uncle's floor. He did feel bad for Uncle D in a way — when he wasn't busy getting goosebumps at the mention of his name. After all, it must have been hard to think such awful things about humanity all the time. Arnold still believed in God — and not only because he was seeing things — but he certainly didn't believe in his *uncle's* god. He avoided church with Ma these days too, but sometimes he listened in at Bethany, the church by the arepa place with a rainbow flag on the door. They seemed to have the right of it, letting people question things on their own and loving them through it all.

His uncle, on the other hand, worshipped a god of hate, an evangelical merchant of death who apparently despised his own creations. But what was the point of that? Why create humans just to smite them? He'd heard the Bible said the word *love* some seven hundred times, while everyone kept whacking each other over the head with a handful of vague verses that didn't really mean anything in the first place. He understood feeling bad about yourself more than anyone, but it was a trap to think pointing out someone else's flaws would fix your own. Only kindness could do that.

"Ah," Uncle D said, opening the door, "Arnold."

The odd thing about his uncle — or all bullies, for that matter — was that he had seemingly forgotten how horrible he'd been to Arnold as a child. Still, Arnold would always be wary of the other man's slow, weighing gaze. Even in his old age, he could lash out at any time with some holy opinion meant to devastate him.

Arnold nodded — trying to calculate how quickly he could drop his bags — when he froze. On his uncle's shoulder was a tiny spirit. Shaped like a child, it floated with its legs crossed, its surface made of inky shadow like obsidian. It spun in a slow circle, though it seemed to be watching Arnold despite a lack of eyes.

"Uh, I have the stuff from Ma," he said, handing over the bag and the little pink box. He didn't have much time to get this right, but if he could capture this spirit, maybe he wouldn't have to show up empty-handed to Nüste's after all. The only problem was the risk. If he accidentally spoke out loud to this spirit, he'd be recommitted to a facility by sundown, no do-overs.

"What are these?" his uncle asked, poking at the macarons in their pink box. Maybe pink and French hadn't been the best choice of peace offering for a man like Uncle D.

"Cookies," he said quickly. "From the place downstairs."

"Blech," his uncle snorted, sticking out his tongue as he put aside the box. "Your mom knows I don't like stuff like that."

"Sorry," Arnold said, leaving the macarons' origins unsaid.

"Anything else?" his uncle asked, looking between Arnold and the door. It seemed they both wanted to be rid of each other. Still, why did the older man have a spirit growing on his shoulder? It could have been an emotion related to seeing Arnold, growing like Jimmy's mountain range, but this tiny spinning doll wasn't going anywhere. It seemed...*a part* of him, a tiny spiritual parrot perched on his shoulder. Against his better judgment, Arnold found himself lingering.

"Uh...no, that's all. Unless *you* need anything? Is...there anything you need done in the apartment?"

His uncle narrowed his eyes as if it were a trap. And maybe it was — not that he planned on telling the older man about the spirit on his shoulder.

"I guess you could look at my sink. I can't get under there anymore."

The apartment wasn't terribly big, a one-bedroom for seniors, though the main room off the doorway had a little kitchenette tucked away to the side. Arnold followed his uncle to the sink, stooping down as he opened the cabinet. There was a little red bucket underneath about half full of water. He watched as a tiny drip came off the pipe. It seemed as if— There were *spirits* under there. He blinked in surprise, watching as a herd of tiny deer no larger than his thumb ran away from the light. They were shimmering and green...mildew spirits maybe? Could he capture those instead?

Arnold was hardly as handy as his father, though he'd been taught enough to avoid being completely useless. He scanned the curve of the sink's pipe, looking for weaknesses. With his uncle looking over his shoulder, though, it felt like being called on in class, a surge of panic rising in him. If he failed to fix the sink after offering the help, he'd never hear the end of it. Still, this was probably the only time he'd have to talk to his uncle — and the spirits — with a captive audience. He decided in that moment he'd capture whichever one talked to him first, taking whatever he could get for Helen.

"I can fix this," he said carefully. "Do you have a wrench?"

"I wonder," his uncle said sarcastically, pointing under the sink. There was a wrench by the bucket, probably sitting there ever since his uncle had tried and failed to fix it.

Arnold chuckled, nodding as he got on his back. "So…how's Chicago treating you?"

"Terrible. No trees. No friends."

"You must miss the mountain."

His uncle scoffed. "How could I not? The city's disgusting. Full of woo-woo losers and criminals."

Seeing spirits probably made Arnold a *woo-woo loser*, so it was lucky he was keeping that to himself.

"Yeah," Arnold said noncommittally.

He worked the wrench against the slip nut on the P-trap. Uncle D might need a new one, the washer a bit rusted with age, but the building could take care of that. Ma kept the super's number taped to her fridge, so he could have her call later. Still, if he could make a little progress on the drip, it'd be a win. He needed to focus on the spirits, though. He glanced at the back of the cabinet, the mildew spirits nowhere to be found. Where had they slipped off to?

I don't have much time, he thought, glancing at the spirit on his uncle's shoulder instead. *But would you want to come to a cafe? For spirits, I mean?*

The spirit swiveled upside down, mimicking Arnold's position under the sink. It cocked its tiny head, continuing its slow orbit around his uncle's shoulder.

Cafe?

"How's your mother?" his uncle asked at the same time.

Arnold almost bit his tongue, his mouth torn between talking with his voice and in his head.

"She's…good?"

"You have to think about it? Your dad not treating her right or something?"

"No, no," Arnold said, straining against the washer. "Just getting this tighter."

Unfortunately, the washer was about as tight as it would go, so his time was nearly up.

It's a cafe for spirits, a place to have coffee and chat, I guess? It's near here. I can…take you?

The spirit giggled, nodding even as it hovered upside down. It began to vibrate, and with a pop of air, it vanished, reappearing on Arnold — though it left a trace behind on Uncle D's shoulder, a sort of afterimage of where it had been before.

"That should do it," he said sitting up. He watched for a moment, and thankfully, the drip didn't come back — yet.

"I'll leave the bucket for now, though. I'll tell the super look at this rusty washer."

"Alright," his uncle said, shutting the cabinets as Arnold stood. "I…thanks, kid."

"Anytime," Arnold said, doing everything he could not to run out the door, spirit in tow.

Chapter Eleven

Nüste kept working away the whole afternoon, managing to get another teacup down. He'd put a chip in the second cup too, unfortunately, but it was a small price to pay to get the cafe running. In the spiritual realm, vessels were incredibly important, and none of this would work without a place to serve the tea.

"That's what you get for forcing me to save you," Nüste grumbled to himself, feeling at the crack in the porcelain with his forehead. If only he—

There was a shift in the air, a familiar energy entering his awareness. *Arnold.* Nüste scrambled out of the box, leaving the teacup for the moment as he hurried back up the window. He didn't think he'd ever be so excited to see that skinny loser, a boy with zero sense for new beginnings. But here he was. Arnold was walking toward the bakery from the train, and he had a spirit on his shoulder. Nüste pushed outward with his awareness, reaching to see what he had brought. It was an unusual spirit to be sure, it was…a *shame* spirit.

Whoa, whoa, whoa! Nüste shouted in his mind, waving his metaphorical arms. Arnold stopped, looking up at the window.

You can talk to me from that far away? Arnold thought, raising an eyebrow.

Sure, I can do whatever I want. But what are you doing? Why would you bring that here? Are you trying to make the poor girl even sadder?

Arnold glanced at the fuzzy orb-like child on his shoulder. *This little guy?*

Why? Isn't this what you told me to do?

Nüste rumpled his forehead, letting out a sigh.

I told you to bring someone worth having tea with. That's a shame spirit! If you thought Helen's confidence was bad before, just wait until that thing gets inside the house. More importantly, they taste terrible!

I... I'm sorry, Arnold thought, looking genuinely pained. His eyes darted between the spirit and Nüste, his hands balled up in fists. *What do I do? We still need spirits, don't we?*

Obviously, but not that kind! Tell him to leave.

Arnold whispered something to the spirit, pointing at the bakery and shaking his head. Nüste couldn't make out what he said. Arnold's psychic link wasn't strong enough yet for his mind and mouth to speak as one — assuming he ever learned, weak-willed as he was. That boy's third eye might as well have an astigmatism, and at this rate they—

The spirit finally nodded, smiling as it drifted off of Arnold's shoulder. It floated higher for a spell before the wind grabbed it, blowing it over the train tracks and out of the neighborhood.

Good riddance! Nüste shouted after it, though the spirit was long gone. He was still plenty mad, though he had to admit — secretly, and only to himself — that he was impressed. Most spirits wouldn't simply leave like that. Perhaps there was hope for Arnold after all, though he couldn't tell the boy that. It would only go to his head, and all of Nüste's hard work would be wasted again. He needed this kid hungry and ready to work.

What do I do now? Arnold asked, still standing on the street.

Leave! Go find me a better spirit!

But...I have something for Helen. It's not a spirit, but what if it helps?

Arnold went into his backpack, pulling out a DVD. He turned it toward the window, as if it meant anything to Nüste. Even worse, it earned him a few looks from passersby. Humans were such fools! They had no ability to focus, their souls like a thousand different spirits jammed inside one body, a storm of useless ideas and hopeless dreams. Of course, that chaos sometimes allowed humans to reach a level of beauty a spirit could only dream of. Perhaps he'd been locked in this attic too long, but he couldn't forget about the wonderful forces of the world that had created him. When they weren't busy being complete and utter pains, humans *could* be something more.

Fine, Nüste thought, trying to make the idea snappish, *but only because she has to get used to seeing you around. Just be quick about it; you're not here to flirt!*

Okay, okay, Arnold thought. He started to cross the street but paused, his foot hanging over the curb. *Wait, did you say that spirit tasted bad?*

———

Helen sat on her stool behind the counter, her head in her hands. An entire afternoon of failed projects were arranged around her, each one a wounded soldier with a hasty bite taken from it. A pan of brownies, a tray of muffins —

there was even a loaf of bread. A feeling had come to her in the shower, something she could only describe as "the pride one feels at no longer smelling bad." It was like lavender, only subtler, as if there were another flavor mixed in, tempering it. She'd actually had some lavender oil she'd made the previous summer, but none of the flavors she'd tried to mask it with felt right.

Vanilla, strawberry, lemon — none of them had made the feeling come back. Was it because she'd sacrificed her freshly showered body on the altar of the baking gods, slamming around the kitchen until her pits began to smell again? At least her deodorant was up to the task. It was a cucumber-melon number she'd grabbed at Eco Flamingo, compostable and everything. Still, even if she wasn't completely rank, four hours of sweating meant she no longer felt the way she had. But that shouldn't matter, right? The whole point of these bakes was to capture the feeling and store it in the flavor. Assuming she wasn't losing her mind.

But what about that guy yesterday? *Arnold*. She could have sworn she'd seen *something* on his face, some sign that everything she'd baked was real. He could have been humoring her, but something in his eyes had given it away. He had felt something, something *she* had baked. If she was really going to run with this, though, it seemed she'd need to become a better baker. Or…feelings-taster, or…whatever. Everything she'd baked today at least *tasted* good, so she may as well fill the case with them. They just weren't *it*. They just didn't have the feeling. Maybe if she—

The bell above the door rang, and she looked up to find Arnold coming through the door. Despite an afternoon full of frustration, she actually smiled. Maybe she was just desperate for someone to prove her theories, but she had a feeling he was more than that too. For one thing, he was nice, and Lord knew she could use more people like that around the shop. Besides, if someone was willing to come back, it meant her baking wasn't as bad as she feared, right? Unless he was back because he…liked her? She shook her head, ignoring the thought. Her life was *way* too out of control to have a boyfriend, handsome or not.

"Hey," he said, waving. "How's it goin'?"

"It's not," she said, motioning at the bakes stacked up behind her. "I couldn't get the flavor right on anything today."

"I mean…it *smells* amazing. What's it supposed to be?"

"Lavender," she said, picking up one of the trays of brownies and putting it on the counter. "I'll give you a free slice to be my guinea pig again."

"No, no, I'm paying. I feel like I owe you after yesterday."

"That good? Or do you just like me or something?"

She wanted to smack herself for that last bit. She'd just had an entirely clear-eyed thought about *not* having room in her life for a boyfriend, and now she was flirting? This place was on his way home and that was that; no sense getting flattered over every repeat customer. Besides, the bakery couldn't afford to have her chasing off the customers. More importantly, if she was being honest with herself, what were the odds he'd come back for a stinky girl with flour in her hair?

"I…uh…well," Arnold stammered, looking like he might jump out the window.

"Only kidding," she said quickly. "Sorry. First rule of business is don't scare the customers."

"No, no," Arnold said, putting his backpack on the counter. "I just hope it's not weird I came back two days in a row. The muffin yesterday was just so good, and the coffee, and… Well, I brought you something as a thank-you. I hope it's alright; just wanted to pay you back with something from *my* work."

Her silly little heart actually *fluttered* at the idea. Why was she such an airhead? With the wrong person, such a move *could* be horribly creepy, but she just didn't get that vibe from Arnold. Besides, gifts were her love language. Even though she knew love languages were pseudo-science far-right propaganda, it was still true. As much as Gran had loved her, her grandmother hadn't been the "words of affirmation" type. Her love had been best expressed through cookies, and there was no chance of changing that now.

Arnold took out a movie from his bag, holding it up before setting it on the counter and sliding it toward her.

"You didn't have to do that!" she said, picking it up. "Your brownie's *definitely* on the house now."

"I do the movies at work. At that record place on Lincoln? I'm not sure if you've seen this one, but it takes place at a bakery, so it made me think of you."

"Yeah, *Kiki's Delivery Service*! I love this movie. I haven't seen it since I was a kid."

"Right?" he said, finally smiling himself. That was a good sign. This wasn't a pretentious gift designed to gate keep her out of the cool kids' club. She'd spent too much of her teens dating jerks like that. No, Arnold genuinely wanted to give it to her, and it showed.

"This is the first one I saw as a kid too, but it tells me something different every time. Miyazaki made it when he was forty-eight, so hopefully I'll never be too old for it."

"You should watch it with me," she said before she could stop herself. She almost bit her tongue for revenge, but it was too late anyway. Arnold looked around, as if a TV might have sprouted somewhere in the bakery.

"Sure, I mean, are you closing soon?"

"I…uh… I mean upstairs. I *live* upstairs. Above the bakery? My roommate's gone tomorrow night if you wanted to come over."

He looked upstairs as if he could see through the ceiling.

"That…would be great. I can bring pizza or something. Or, well, I guess maybe you're sick of bread and stuff after baking all day?"

"Pizza's great," she said, smiling. "It's crust, so it's like, way different."

Maybe this wouldn't be such an awful idea after all. She could always use a friend, right? She'd hardly met anyone since moving back to Chicago — and Em and her awful boyfriend didn't count.

He laughed. He wasn't pretentious and he didn't mind funny women? Who was this guy and where had Chicago been hiding him?! Not that she cared. He was just a friend.

"What time?"

"How's seven? It'll give me time to look presentable after I close tomorrow."

"You look plenty presentable now," he said, though that was a little generous based on her reflection in the glass case. "What do you like on your pizza?"

"Oh, anything!"

That was better. Casual, normal. She took a deep breath, trying to reset her nerves. Forcing a smile to her face, she reached for a clean plate.

"Now, about that brownie…"

Chapter Twelve

The next morning, Arnold left early, hoping he could find a better spirit to offer Nüste. Sundays were basically his only free day, and with a mountain of homework to do before seeing Helen, he needed to get going. He started heading east, crossing under the Brown Line as the train rumbled overhead.

He turned left at Ravenswood, walking along the Metra tracks as one of the giant double-decker trains rushed past on its way to the suburbs. Former factories rose around him, their smokestacks and clock towers standing vigil even though their work was long done. A few people wandered the public gardens that ran along the train, clearing out the old weeds for spring. A class was getting out of the Lillistreet Art Center too, a handful of women showing off their pottery fresh from the kiln.

There was always so much happening in the city, hundreds of thousands of lives unfolding at their own pace. It was hard to put his finger on why, but it fed him somehow, making him feel a part of things, even if he was the same old Arnold living in his little studio. Maybe he was just another spirit, drawn toward the energy of the people all around him.

He kept heading north until he reached Roseland Cemetery, the gate and its guardhouse like something from another time. The cemetery was on nearly four hundred acres, an inconceivable wealth of land to set aside now. It was founded before the Civil War, when Edgewater was still a beach town and not just another neighborhood in a massive city. It even had its own herd of deer, a few dozen of them somehow still hemmed in by the fences, chewing on the arborvitae to pass the time.

He stopped by the gate as he passed, looking out at the sea of mausoleums. There were none of the little candle flame spirits he'd seen at the cemetery by school; the ancient spirits buried here no doubt moved on long ago. Still, there was something he'd never noticed before. On some of the gravestones, there were huge clumps of moss, a mass of spongy green clinging to the tops and reaching down the sides. Perhaps he wouldn't have thought they were spirits before, but after seeing the dust creature at work, every remotely blob-shaped object was suspect.

He decided to turn in, heading for the closest patch of graves. There were a handful of runners weaving along the paths. Would it feel strange to go running in a cemetery? He admittedly wasn't a great exerciser himself, but it seemed a bit like showing off to the dead. *Look at me, still sucking down air, running around!* Even worse, he'd been the kind of kid who held his breath driving past cemeteries growing up — though the Western Avenue edge of Rosehill, which was almost a mile long, was always too much for him. He could walk in a cemetery just fine now, but heaving in lungfuls of ghosts on a run? It felt…precarious.

He glanced around, though no one was near him when he stepped up to the first patch of moss. The moment he got close, two giant eyes appeared, making him jump. Unlike Poppyseed or the dust spirit, though, the eyes didn't seem fixed. They drifted, floating like bits of pasta in a green soup.

Interesting, the spirit thought, its voice low and grumbling like thunder.

I could say the same, Arnold thought. Was that too mouthy? He didn't know what kind of spirit this was. He *was* getting more comfortable around them, though that wasn't necessarily a good sign for his mental state. *What…are you?*

Every soul has dreams, it said, its eyes swiveling away from Arnold to face the sky. *Some more than others, but humans the most. They strive, shaping the world around them. And yet, they die. When they pass on, their dreams stay behind.*

You're…the left-behind dreams of the dead?

The eyes turned back to him, though they overshot, bouncing off the edge of the moss as their momentum carried them forward. He didn't mind talking to this spirit — it was strangely calming — though he ought to find a polite way to end the conversation soon. After the dressing down Nüste had given him for the shame spirit, he'd hardly get a hero's welcome for bringing back a clump of broken dreams.

No, the spirit said simply. *Dreams, yes, but not exclusively of the dead.*

But— Arnold started as the spirit laughed, its jolly sound ringing in his mind.

Don't look so glum, child human. Dreams are a force, like sunlight, merely borrowed for a time. I live on in each new dreamer's mind, a piece of me disappearing once the dream is shared. The human buried here simply dreamed too much, and it has taken time for me to float away. But I am making progress.

When I first appeared here, I covered the whole grave!

The grave was marked 1892 for a woman named Clara. It was enormous, the chunk of reddish marble easily four feet wide.

"What was her dream?" Arnold whispered, forgetting to speak it in his mind.

To help the poor, I think. A worthy dream, both sad and encouraging. The poor are still with you, I gather. And yet, each year, pieces of myself still float away as humankind fights on. Perhaps one day they'll reach their goal and I'll be naught but sunlight.

When the spirit put it like that, it didn't *sound* sad. Still, he didn't want to cross Nüste again. The little mushroom man may be small, but he was awfully fierce. He had to try, though, right? What if he brought a backup? The shame spirit had ridden on his shoulder the day before, and he had two shoulders he could use. What if he brought this spirit as a backup and kept looking? Would it come with him? The dust spirit hadn't had the slightest interest, even in an attic filled with dust.

This might be an odd question, but would you be interested in going to a cafe?

——

An hour later, Arnold was finally heading home, *two* spirits perched on his shoulders. If anyone else could see them, he probably looked like a general in an army of the absurd, the green and brown blobs like epaulets on his shirt. In the end, the moss spirit hadn't minded coming at all, lending Arnold a fragment of her spirit — assuming it was a she like Clara. Apparently, Clara's Dream could go anywhere she chose, there simply wasn't much reason to leave the quiet of the graveyard if she would dissipate on her own.

His other choice had been obvious. He couldn't leave Poppyseed behind, not when he'd asked *specifically* for a cafe. The spirit's usefulness to Helen might be questionable, but she *was* a baker. If anyone was going to have a pure feeling about a bagel, it'd be her. Besides, hadn't Poppyseed said he was attracted to longing? He hadn't questioned Nüste much about what it was exactly that Helen needed, but having a bakery must be hard. *He'd* certainly never done anything that brave. Longing might not be what she was looking for, but it couldn't hurt.

Luckily, Poppyseed had just as easily detached a piece of himself to come with Arnold, though it hadn't worked in quite the same way. Whereas Clara's Dream had brought only a piece of herself, the bagel seemed to have transferred his entire consciousness. Both of Poppyseed's eyes sat perched on Arnold's shoulder, looking out at the world. The moss spirit, on the other hand, was a blank clump of green, her eyes only occasionally drifting into view. It was like the bit on his shoulder was still connected to the mass on the grave, letting Clara's dream enter in and out of Arnold's segment of the space-time continuum.

As he came up to his building, he headed for the alley, walking around back, where he might slip upstairs unnoticed. He was getting better at only talking to spirits in his mind, but was it really worth interacting with his neighbors if he didn't have to? More importantly, he had a few hours to kill before leaving for Helen's, and he needed to find a way to get the spirits off his shoulders for a bit without installing themselves in his studio. Beyond not wanting those eyes watching him as he slept, the landlord would kill him if he started a spiritual infestation.

We're gonna go inside for a bit, he thought to them, slipping past the garbage cans. *If I run into someone, try not to talk to me. I'm...not sure I'll be able to multitask like that.*

Getting Poppyseed had been risky enough. The same girl had been working the register as last time, and she'd given him a hell of a strange look. After all, it had only been a few days since his first experience with the bagel spirit — even if it felt like a lifetime ago with the rollercoaster he'd been on. He'd ordered something complicated, picking the sandwich with the most ingredients. Luckily, it had been enough to pull her off the register, giving him just enough time to get the spirit on his shoulder.

Is the cafe inside? Poppyseed asked, his voice strangely higher-pitched once it had been separated from his larger body.

Er...no, Arnold said pausing at the back gate. *We'll be going soon, though. I just have a few things to do first.*

He didn't exactly feel like explaining to a spirit that he had homework. Did spirits even have to learn, or did they just know things?

Very well, the bagel spirit said with a huff. *This...establishment will do for now. But if I'm not in a cafe by nightfall, you'll be sorrier than a triple-cheddar cream cheese.*

Arnold didn't ask what that meant, reaching for his house keys as he rushed through the alley. But if a bagel spirit only spoke in bagel threats, it couldn't imply anything good. He just hoped the afternoon went quickly, toppings not included. He—

"Arnold!" a voice called. He looked up, finding Lois looking down at him from the roof. "It's time to garden, sweetie. Hurry on up."

Shit, he thought. Hanging out with Lois was *his* idea, and he'd forgotten. Now, he'd have to do it with a bunch of spirits on his back.

When Arnold reached the building's top floor, he found the access ladder pulled down in the middle of the hallway. It was a wonder Lois could climb it at her age, but she was much tougher than she looked. It didn't scream "the landlord doesn't mind if you do this," but he'd been up there plenty of times to carry her supplies without getting in trouble.

I need you guys to keep quiet for a little bit, alright? I promise we'll leave for the cafe soon.

Clara's dream didn't answer; she just let her eye wander in and out of its mossy frame. Poppyseed grunted his agreement, which seemed like...progress?

Up on the roof, the white tar-patch shining in the sun, Arnold stopped for a second to look at the view. Living on the northwest side, it was easy to forget how close he was to the city's massive skyscrapers. From the roof, though, you could see them all, the Hancock and the Sears — he refused to call them anything else — glinting on the horizon.

"Boy, was I glad to see you," Lois said, waving at him with a trowel in hand. "I thought you forgot."

He *had* forgotten, but he kept that to himself as he wandered over. She'd set up a half-dozen raised beds — the soil had been murder to get up the ladder — and she was scraping the dirt around, smoothing it out. She had lined the beds with twine, dividing them into sections.

"What are we doing?"

She paused, cocking her head as she looked at him. "Is there something different about you? Your hair?"

"No?" he asked, glancing at the spirits on his shoulders.

Lois shrugged. "Well, get me more of that topsoil," she said, pointing at the pile of bags behind her. "Today we're organizing. But in a couple weeks, we plant! I want these babies humming by May."

Picking up the heavy soil, his muscles groaned. He *felt* like someone who survived off of fortune cookies. Still, he was happy to do it for Lois. She was his first friend, and for once, he was actually useful to someone else.

"These are going to be cucumbers," she said, pointing to the first section. "And those will be tomatoes. Why don't you spread that in the last bed."

Lois had tied her white hair into braids, and she was humming to herself. She kneeled on a gardening pad with the Bears logo on it, though the dark blue and orange was faded from years in the sun.

"Can I ask you a question?" he asked, shaking the soil out of the bag.

"Sure, sweetie. The old don't bother with secrets. Not worth the time."

"Do you…believe in spirits?"

"Like ghosts?"

"Kind of? I think?"

I'm not a ghost, Poppyseed chirped from his shoulder. *I already told you that. It's like you don't even—*

Arnold shushed the bagel spirit in his mind.

"I sure do! My husband visits me every night. He thought he could die on me, but I've trapped him."

"Is that what your dreamcatchers are for?"

"Among other things," she said. She looked at him, smiling. "Why do you ask? Did you…lose somebody too?"

"Nothing like that. Just curious. I…" Well, the truth was better left unsaid. "What was your husband like?"

Lois sighed, though she smiled again after.

"He was a wonderful man. Bit of a fool — always forgetting things — but he was *my* fool. Actually, you kind of remind me of him. He was always wearing glasses and bumping into things."

Arnold wasn't sure that was a compliment, but if Lois could love someone similar, maybe there was hope for him after all.

"I drove him nuts too, always embarrassing him at the church potlucks. Called me a 'stubborn mule' more times than I can count, but that's what he liked about me, I think. He was meek as all get-out. I used to fight his battles for him. Still do, actually. You should see the state of his grave! I gave the manager an earful last time…"

As Lois kept talking, Arnold felt something shift on his left shoulder. He looked down, finding Clara's dream floating back into view.

I bet her husband had delicious dreams, the spirit said. *I wonder what cemetery he's at…*

"What cemetery is your husband at?" Arnold asked when there was a pause in Lois's story — if only to keep his brain from splitting as he tried to think two things at once.

"St. Henry's," she said. "My husband was a Croat Catholic. Gave my parents a fit — they were Baptists."

"I'd love to join you next time. Uh…if that's not weird?"

"Not at all, sweetie. My grandkids all flew the coop, so no one ever comes with me. You're a good egg, aren't you?"

He found himself glowing under the praise. It was probably the kind of thing grandmothers said to everyone his age. Still, it poked at something dormant in his heart, something he'd forgotten since everything fell apart out east.

Well, Poppyseed said from his shoulder, *at least you're not a completely terrible host! It dissipated rather quickly, but the feeling you just had was delectable. Self-esteem, maybe? Almost as good as a cafe, if I do say so myself.*

"Go get another bag, will you?" Lois asked.

Arnold sprang up, eager to do whatever it took to keep that feeling from disappearing.

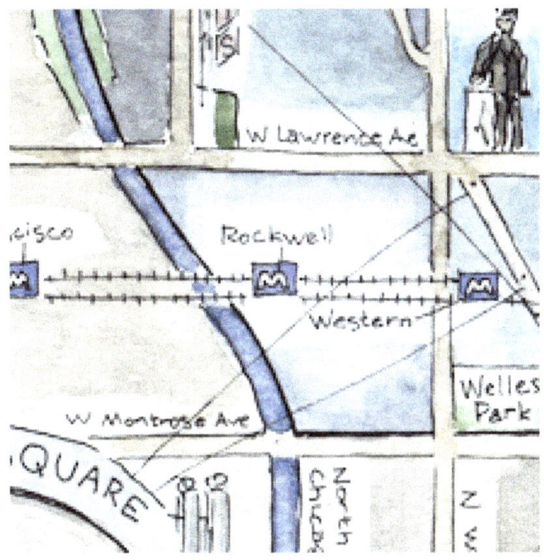

Chapter Thirteen

Helen stopped in the middle of the kitchen, blowing the hair from her eyes. Her mind was all over the place. She only had two hours until Arnold arrived, and she was still trying to bake something for him, clean the living room, hide everything incriminating in her apartment, *and* pick up a bottle of wine. It was the kind of to-do list that made her head spin — and something she normally tried to escape through baking.

Unfortunately, when things were this high-stakes, even baking didn't help. She'd piled up every ingredient she had on the counter and still had no idea what she wanted to make. She wanted it to be *special*, but what did that mean? Baking was a blend of tradition and inspiration, and barring something Arnold had never tried before, was that really capable of blowing his mind? She could try to bake a feeling, but she hadn't really *felt* anything today. Unless you counted the usual drudgery of running a failing business.

She leaned against the counter, closing her eyes. She pictured Arnold coming into the shop, his dorky little smile, pizza in hand. Her heart *fluttered*, doing a little somersault. Ignoring her instinct to quash such feelings — this was *not* a date — she held on, trying to harness its power. There was *something* there. She tried to feel it in her body, focusing on the somatic work she'd started doing back in Boston — when the stress of her post-college baking gig had made her hair start falling out. She followed the butterflies to their source, the little cocoon in her stomach where they'd burrowed away, waiting for a chance to come out.

"I know you," she whispered to them, tracking each breath as it blew past the crop of butterflies.

Suddenly, in her mind's eye, she saw herself in a dress. A fancy gown. Midnight blue, it draped over her curves, hugging and hiding them in perfect measure. She could feel makeup on her face, a foreign luxury in a bakery, the warmth of the lights shining against it. Her ankles ached from the heels she was wearing. She could almost hear the rumble of a crowd around her, whispers and laughs jockeying for position even as a DJ's music thumped nearby.

This was a memory, right? It was…the President's Ball, back in school, one of the only times she'd ever seen her classmates out of their chef's hats. It was like prom — only with way more drinking — though a certain…anticipation about it felt the same. She hadn't had a date that night, but she'd wanted — no, *needed* — to look her best, self-conscious and confident in equal measure.

As the memory slid into place, she finally tasted its flavor, the pieces of it prickling across her tongue like lightning. Her eyes burst open, and she reached for a pen. *Chocolate ganache, cacao nibs, raspberry*, she wrote in quick succession. Somehow, she knew she could put those flavors in almost anything and likely preserve the feeling, though they felt more suited to a cupcake. There was something about a cupcake's fluffiness that matched the feeling. There was also the tiniest trace of something hiding on the back of her tongue, some secret ingredient gluing it all together…

"Masala!" she shouted, barreling around the counter and dashing upstairs. That wasn't something she kept in the bakery, but she knew she had some in her apartment. As she began to feel the bake unfolding in her mind — the way a choreographer must feel when they simply *knew* the steps — she also had a sinking feeling she wouldn't have time to wash her hair. A bit ironic for a "prom cake." Still, if she got the flavors right, it would hardly matter. A way to a man's heart was through his stomach anyway, right? Even if entering another man's heart was the last thing she wanted.

———

Arnold stepped off the train, the bakery shining like a beacon from across the street. Like most spring nights, it was dark and blustery, and it felt like the lighthouse he needed, his only hope on his spiritually stormy seas — especially with the cargo he was carrying.

After gardening with Lois, his studying hadn't been…*particularly* productive. Poppyseed had started talking the moment they got inside his apartment, making it impossible to read more than a sentence of his textbook at a time. Still, none of that could dim his sense of accomplishment. Not only had he collected two spirits, but he'd harbored them long enough to reach the bakery. Now, he just had to hope Nüste would let them in.

He still had an entire movie night with Helen to worry about — a dreamlike possibility he never would have even considered just two days ago — but even that would mean little if he didn't do his part in helping her. After all, that's why he was letting himself hang around, wasn't it? Anything else, any other *delusion*, would only be doing Helen a disservice. This most certainly *wasn't* a date. He was probably the most uniquely un-date-worthy person in Chicago, epithet-wielding Wiener's Circle employees included.

Nüste! he thought as loudly as he could, stopping just across the street from the bakery.

The spirits on his shoulders stirred — responding to his "mind-voice," as he'd taken to calling it. One of the moss spirit's eyes returned as Poppyseed opened his.

Are we here? Poppyseed asked. *Finally! I was starting to think you'd spirit-napped me. An incredibly cruel thing to do, by the way, it—*

Arnold? Nüste called, his little mushroom form appearing in the window. *Arnold! You did it! Not bad, my young, hapless friend. Not bad at all. These are excellent customers. How do you do, friends? Welcome to Nüste's Spirit Cafe!*

Hapless was going a little far, but Arnold still felt oddly pleased with himself — especially having avoided another screw-up — though the shame spirit *had* forced him to consider some very hard, sad truths about his uncle.

How should I drop them off? he asked, pausing on the curb. He looked around for a fire escape or something — though the last thing he wanted in this world was for Helen to catch him climbing up the outside of her building.

Just let go, Nüste thought back. *I can see the part of your soul anchoring our treasured guests. Release it, and I'll catch them with my own.*

Arnold closed his eyes, feeling for the spirits with his mind. Oddly, he *could* feel the contours of the small creatures, a sort of border between where he ended and they began. And on that border — in a not-at-all comforting way — there *was* a sort of attachment, the anchor Nüste must have been referring to. He didn't love the idea of their souls being linked to his, but at least it was time for them to leave. He pried at the connection with his mind, though it didn't give way.

Let. Go. Nüste thought. *Release, don't pry. The soul isn't a crowbar.* Nüste grumbled something inaudibly after that, though it didn't sound like a compliment.

Release. Right. Arnold went deeper, feeling where the anchor touched his soul. And he just…let go, feeling it dissolve as he imagined the spirits floating away like balloons. And they *did* sort of float in a way. They moved toward Nüste, floating like dandelion fluff sucked into a vacuum. For a moment, he was worried they'd get dragged away by the wind or something, but as they touched the bakery, they *dissolved* somehow, reappearing on the other side of the window.

Job well done, Nüste thought, giving a sort of mushroom-man bow to his new guests. *I'll take care of our lovely new friends. You work on not screwing up movie night, Romeo.*

Romeo. Arnold gulped, crossing the street. Odd, after everything he'd been through that afternoon, that this part should feel like the real gamble, but it did.

Capturing a bunch of spiritual blobs was one thing. Meeting up with a beautiful woman several hundred thousand miles out of his league was quite another. He opened the door to the bakery, the bell tinkling as he stepped into the light.

He'd told her she didn't need to dress up — and she hadn't exactly — but she was somehow even more immaculate than last time, an angel of baking with a spatula instead of a sword. She wore a sweater, something vintage, by the look of it. Its purple wool was studded with sparkles, each one twinkling like a tiny planet swirling around her sun. Helen looked up, smiling as she noticed him, a thousand volts coursing through him at the sight.

Relax, he told himself — praying the thought wouldn't stray into his mind-voice toward Nüste and his guests. *Just a new friend having me over for a movie night. Totally normal.* Of course, he didn't have many gorgeous friends who ran their own bakeries. The smell alone was intoxicating, like the chocolate factory they used to operate downtown, each breath filling him with sweetness.

"Hey," he said with a wave, though he stayed standing by the door. He still felt oddly like a customer. "Do you want me to lock it?" he asked. "You're closed, right?"

"That'd be great, thanks," she said, finishing frosting something with a flourish. "No pizza?"

"Uh…delivery," he said doing the bolt on the door. "I guess they'll call me? I know Jimmy's is close, but I didn't want it to get cold walking from the train." Or, you know, interfere with the two spirits he'd deposited in her attic…

"Works for me," she said, coming over with a tray full of perfect-looking cupcakes. "Why don't I show you around and we can crack open the wine?"

"Perfect," he said, gesturing for her to lead the way.

She did a little curtsey with her cupcake tray, taking him through a door on the right. It led to a stairwell and a back door, apparently the path up to her apartment. He glanced out the little pane window, noticing a square box on the concrete out back, whirring in the darkness.

"Is that a heat pump?" he asked. He left out the nerdy part of asking if it was a Mitsubishi i3, capable of handling temperatures down to -13 degrees. But she lit up anyway, spinning back around to face him on the stairs.

"It is! Are you a climate nerd like me?"

"Maybe an aspiring one," he said, laughing. "I did a project at my old school, a commercial for a local dealer. They're pretty sick, though!"

"Well, my friend, you've come to the right place. Hold this." She handed him the cupcakes, pulling up her sweater. Beneath it was a bright green T-shirt emblazoned with a unit much like the one out back. Underneath, it was bedazzled with the words "Get a F*cking Heat Pump."

I think I'm in love, he almost said, swallowing the words at the last second. He would only be joking — in a way — but that almost certainly wouldn't have come out right.

"I think this is the greatest bakery in the world," he said instead, feeling like he might burst into flames.

"Yeah, yeah," she said, smiling as she took the tray back. "Come with me.

You can bask in the heat pump's glorious warmth upstairs."

He trailed behind her, feeling oddly sweaty for having just come in from outside. He still didn't know what to do with himself, but pizza, *Kiki's Delivery Service*, and tray full of cupcakes wasn't a bad place to start. No matter what came of this night, "glorious warmth" certainly felt like the right word for it.

Chapter Fourteen

Nüste scurried across the attic floor, preparing tea for his guests. Even though Arnold had only brought a shoulderful of each spirit, they had puffed up inside, squeezing more of their souls into the space as they spread out among the boxes. They were chatting to each other, filling the air with the hum of spiritual energy. At least Arnold had done better this time. These two were a bit rare as far as spirits went, but their base natures — hope and longing — would be more useful to Helen than a sodding *shame spirit.*

Nüste had spent the night before scraping emotions off the attic's ceiling, and now he was sweeping them up in a hurry — ideally before his customers got impatient and left. Soon, he had quite a pile going, the emotions like glowing snow. It was made up of all the things Helen — and presumably her roommate — had been feeling lately. It was sort of a hodgepodge, but what about humans wasn't? He pushed his pile against the teapot in the center of the room, heaving with his entire essence until the emotions fell in, melting together as a swirl in the porcelain.

He couldn't guarantee the flavor based on what he had available, but spirits often had eclectic tastes. These two would likely enjoy whatever he came up with, anything to provide some variety to their existence. The spirits Arnold had found were old, and they'd probably grown tired of waiting for something to happen, for someone to talk to.

Precisely, the moss spirit grumbled, agreeing with whatever the bagel hole had said.

Nüste shivered at the thought of ever becoming like these two. He was old himself, true, but he'd never been *stuck* like them. Spirits like these were anchored by design, drawn to solid things. Nüste, on the other hand, was from the family of *Ephemera*, their stodgy way of life anathema to him. Unfortunately, his time in the attic had also taught him just how similar all spirits were. If Nüste, a titan of beginnings, could get stuck, then anyone could. It made him work faster, desperate to begin the process of setting himself free. If he failed, he'd be wishing he could be something as simple as a bagel.

Nearly ready! he called out to his customers, watching as the glowing pot began to bubble over. It wouldn't look like anything to human eyes, but he'd gotten quite the brew going. Putting this many stray emotions together was volatile, and if he didn't serve it hot, it may well boil over. It wouldn't hurt the customers — these spirits were too hearty for that — but receiving a faceful of overcooked human emotions could be…unpleasant.

He willed the spiritual drink from its vessel, the raw emotional power darting from the teapot to the cups he'd set up around the room. Eventually, he'd be able to serve as many as a dozen customers, each cup like a table in a human cafe. It had been quite an undertaking to move them all, but with spirits, it wasn't like he'd need to wash them. The cups could at least stay where they were for the foreseeable future.

As the drinks landed, the spirits ceased their conversation — which was a tiny miracle, given how much the bagel liked the sound of his own voice.

Fascinating, Poppyseed murmured. *Why, this is just the thing! You know, after so many years stuck in the shop, it's a wonder to try something new.*

Sure, sure, Nüste said. *Enjoy it while it's hot.*

The moss spirit, thankfully, was nowhere near as verbose. It probably took a good deal of patience to sit on a gravestone waiting for dreams to be dreamt. Bagels, by contrast, were always flying out the door, every day another dozen. It was a wonder such a permanent spirit had grown up around something edible. A bit ironic that, seeing as how he was trapped in a bakery…

Nüste leaned against a box, watching as his customers "sipped" their tea. This was the critical part of the process, the moment when his work would — *hopefully* — start paying off. At first, the tea seemed to do nothing, slipping inside the spirits like a drink inside a person. Most spirits were at least a bit translucent, so he could see when the glowing soup of emotions appeared on the inside. Drifting through their blob-like frames, the drinks *globulized*, floating like liquid in a lava lamp. Nüste could imagine the tingle they were feeling, each bead of color like a tiny flame, the power of the human spirit raging inside.

Delectable, the bagel said, closing his eyes. *It's almost like being one of them! What a flavor you've compiled, dear Nüste. Delectable indeed!*

Uh…it's my pleasure, Nüste thought, giving a tiny bow with his mushroom cap head. Where did this bagel get off being so posh? Weren't bagels some poor man's food from an 1800s shtetl? They'd risen in stature over the years, true, but it was a hell of a way to speak for a spirit that could be covered in "schmear" at any moment.

Still…he wasn't all bad. You knew a hateful spirit when you saw one, and this bagel didn't have a spiteful bone in his boneless little body. Spirits simply were the way they were. You'd have an easier time blaming the wind for blowing.

Something *shifted* in the spirits, the volatile energy of the human emotions absorbing into the spiritual energy of their hosts. In a way, it was like human digestion. It let off a bit of light and heat in the process, but the most important part — the part that mattered to Nüste — was the final byproduct.

As the spirits absorbed their new "nutrients," the displaced bits of their former selves began to rise. Like bubbles in a pond, they floated higher and higher until they popped out the top of each spirit, escaping as *new* emotions. Hope and longing, they fluttered like gaseous butterflies until they hit the ceiling, where they blended with the others, a pinkish haze dancing over the wooden beams. *That* was what he had to offer Helen with this little cafe. Just like her emotions floating up, the ones he collected would float *down*, working their way into her psyche. If he could find an emotion that would inspire her to climb up to the attic, he'd be free.

He stood, watching the swirling feelings with pride. Hope and longing were simplifications, of course, human words for something more eternal. But that was like the name Nüste itself. It hid a *network* of meaning beyond human understanding. He knew humans thought that way on the inside, beyond their awareness, the abstractions building upon each other until they reached some approximation of the truth.

If he were to *truly* translate the moss spirit's feeling, for example, it would be something like "the feeling of possibility one feels when their designs seem realizable, not only in the sense of accomplishing them but of feeling they are dreams worth dreaming, and that in some small way, even a finite human can achieve a fraction of the heavens they glimpsed in their subconscious mind."

But sure, the word *hope* was fine too. Luckily for him, Helen seemed to have a unique ability to harness the purity of feelings. The things he'd felt floating up from the bakery were highly specific, each baked good brimming with potential like an atom waiting to fuse to another. And being able to extend those feelings from her own soul into her baking… Well, it was rare indeed — far rarer than what Arnold could do. Even so, finding two spiritual humans in the same place was really something. Maybe they really *were* meant for each other.

A bit more if you would! the bagel spirit called, the equivalent of a human tapping their cup for a refill.

Sure, sure, Nüste said, hopping down to the floor so he could scrape up more feelings. There was a limit to how much he'd be able to serve in a single session — dependent mainly on how many feelings Helen shed each week — though he could certainly oblige this first request. He certainly didn't want a reputation for being stingy. He wanted his reputation to spread, to get as many customers as he could, each one a cobblestone on his path to freedom.

Just keep 'em coming, Arnold, he thought, sensing the kid downstairs. *Keep 'em coming.*

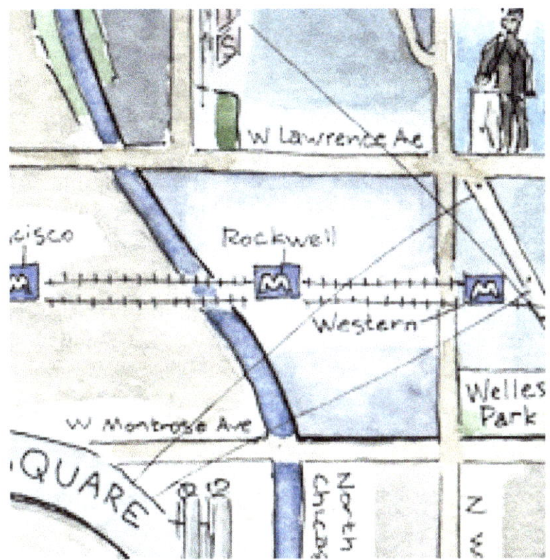

Chapter Fifteen

Arnold looked down into his wine, the liquid like a purple ocean trying to escape the glass. One side even had a tiny spirit in it. It looked like a grapevine, stretching up the sides. It seemed like what Nüste had called a "passive spirit," one without a mind, attracted to the nature of the wine itself. That meant it wouldn't be useful to the cafe, which was probably just as well. It was alien, reaching out like a tentacle from a horror movie.

"How's the wine?" Helen asked, coming back to the couch with her own glass.

"Great," Arnold said, carefully taking a sip from the side *without* a spirit growing in it. He was on too many meds to be drinking much, but hopefully his tiny sips wouldn't offend Helen. She was obviously passionate about flavor, and from the way she'd gushed about the wine — a Sangiovese — her passion seemed to extend beyond baking. Actually, shouldn't he be complimenting her on that? The only good advice Arnold had ever heard about dating was to "put your thoughts on the outside" — even though he would never presume to be *dating* Helen.

"It's impressive how much you know about flavor. Did you go to culinary school?"

"Unfortunately," she said, rolling her eyes, though she still somehow looked pleased at the compliment. "I went to Johnson & Wales, if you've heard of it. It was an expensive nightmare, but I guess it taught me some things."

"Whoa, you were in Providence? I went to RISD for a little while!"

"No kidding," she said, raising her glass. "Not many of us get out of P-town.

It's like Boston—"

"Except worse," they both said at the same time, making her laugh. And it sort of was — all the gritty East Coast feel with double the mob presence. Still, he remembered the water being beautiful, the Providence River running into the Seekonk and wrapping its arms around everything. The people were interesting too, everyone making or doing something. They *were* kind of mean, but wasn't everywhere on the East Coast like that? He felt more at home in the Midwest, more at ease. There was less pressure to *impress* everyone all the time, but it was also hard to separate coming home from abandoning his dreams.

"RISD's a big deal," Helen said, clinking his glass. "What did you study?"

"Animation," he said as if it were an apology, gesturing at the TV where the DVD menu was playing in a beautiful, endless loop. The sad music didn't really seem right for a non-date date, but it *was* gorgeous, the minor chords rising and falling like Kiki's broom.

"Ahhh," she said, nodding as she sipped her wine. "Smart *and* creative, a dangerous combination."

"Takes one to know one," he said, trying to slip free of the compliment as he picked up one of Helen's cupcakes. Apparently made just for him, they were chocolate with swirls of pink frosting. She'd even made little pictures with the sprinkles on top — smiley faces, shoes, top hats.

"I really don't know how you do it with these. The flavor is…"

He took a bite, closing his eyes. Just like the muffin she gave him the other day, it was the oddest thing. The flavor hit him as a *memory* — in this case, getting ready for prom. He could picture Ma hovering around him, fixing his boutonniere. He had gone with a friend, so he hadn't been feeling butterflies exactly. But there had still been a certain *excitement* about looking fancy on purpose, about waiting for an event all day and wondering how it would go.

"Sorry if this is weird, but it tastes like…prom, I guess? Like getting ready for something fancy. Maybe it's the top hats."

"That's exactly it!" she yelled, clapping her hands together. "Hold on." She pulled out her phone, typing furiously. "I just need to make some notes, I'm…working on something."

"Not more poison, right?"

She laughed, smacking him on the knee and sending a tingle up his spine. He loved how *breezy* she was, how comfortable she was in her own skin. He could never pull off a casual knee smack. It would be too loaded, too creepy. Of course, with how magnetic she was, it was worth remembering that the gesture almost certainly meant nothing. Some people were just better at being themselves. It was a compliment that she was comfortable around him, sure, but nothing more. He had to remind himself for the thousandth time — this was *not* a date.

"Okay, sorry," she finally said, smiling as she put down her phone, her face like a sunbeam. It was a wonder he didn't conjure up one of those "pure feeling" spirits from her face alone. "But I'm not letting you get away that easy. Tell me more about your animation."

"Not much to tell, I'm afraid. I ended up switching schools so I could come home."

"Psychology, right? That's cool. Do you still animate, though? Or do you have anything I can see?"

"There's a couple things on YouTube, I guess. Short projects from school and stuff, nothing special."

"Okay, Mr. YouTube," she said with a grin, opening her phone again. He felt his stomach flip over at the prospect of her looking at his shoddy work. Also, he *really* didn't want to seem like he was bragging. After all, what was there to brag about? He was a dropout with a handful of seven-second clips, nothing more.

It reminded him of a podcast he'd listened to in class with Agnes Callard. He couldn't remember all of it, but she'd basically said conversations with new people have three forms — sharing the basics about your lives, subtly jockeying for status, and "leveling," which was basically coming clean about the ways you aren't that special. That might not apply to this, but the last thing he wanted was for Helen to think he was pompous — or even worse, *hitting on her* with some big East Coast ego he didn't have. It was probably too vulnerable for someone he'd just met, but if he tried to level with her, maybe she would see the real him.

"It's not a flex," he said quickly, "*really*. I flamed out at school. I only made it to my second year before coming home. It was…too stressful, I guess."

"Hey, at least you tried," she said, giving him a sad smile. She sighed, putting down her phone to stare into her wine. "Everybody's so obsessed with being great, but what does that even mean? Who decides? Your teachers? Your boss? It might make me lose my bakery, but if I'm not doing what I love, I'll scream." She picked up one of her cupcakes, biting off the top. "Even if it's silly."

"It's not silly," he said. "It's…delicious."

She stared into the cupcake, thoughtful. "It *is* that, at least."

"You ever heard of Plato's *Republic*?" he asked. It seemed all he was good for was citing schoolwork, but what she'd said had actually reminded him of it.

"Vaguely," she said. "It's the metal heart thing, right?"

"Yeah! It's like what you were saying about being great. Everyone in the utopia is born with a single metal in their heart, and it decides what they're allowed to be. But, I don't know…can't we be more than that? Can't we be ordinary *and* great? I'd rather eat a thousand cupcakes of yours than be some hot shot anyway."

Helen laughed, cheersing what was left of his cupcake with hers.

"Amen to that. Though you might get sick of me before you hit the thousand mark."

"Only one way to find out."

As he ate the rest of the cupcake, a different memory came to him, one from a cousin's wedding. Still, it was oddly similar, the memory of him putting a suit on.

"You know," she said, "I have a friend from high school who's always posting about her animation club. They meet at a library around here. Would you want me to introduce you?"

"I…" He thought of all the notebooks he hadn't touched since school, the pencils he could hardly stand to hold. With all the exposures he'd successfully done in therapy, he still hadn't done any art. Still, something in her face made him feel like saying yes. He felt like he might be able to believe in *anything* if Helen believed in it first. "That'd be great, actually."

"Great," she said, picking up the remote. "Now, you look sufficiently mortified, so I'm gonna start this movie. But when we're done, I'm watching every YouTube video you have while you lecture me on the art form. Deal?"

She raised her eyebrows, giving him one last chance at escape, though it wasn't really a question.

"Deal," he said, taking another bite of his cupcake. He wanted to be here. He wanted to taste like prom. And for the first time in a while, he wanted to be himself.

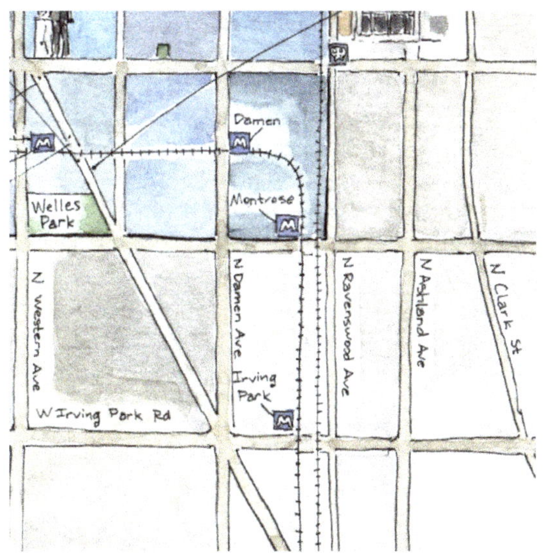

Chapter Sixteen

The next day, Helen left the bakery, zipping up her jacket. It was sunny and unseasonably warm, but the wind was whipping, pulling giant blimp-like clouds along at an unforgiving pace. It was, essentially, the type of day she'd been euphemistically calling "new spring." One day it would be twenty degrees, the next day sixty, thunderstorms rolling into snow that gave way to sun. It would be beautiful if it weren't so terrifying, yet another harbinger of a rapidly changing climate.

"You're doing what you can," she said, whispering her mantra to herself, crossing the street toward the Brown Line.

And for once in her life, it felt like she was. She was electrifying the bakery, composting, eating less meat. Maybe it was a small contribution compared to scientists and engineers, but somebody had to actually *use* all the cool stuff the more talented folks were making. The key was to stay hopeful. Despair would only cause paralysis, and good things *were* happening. Ninety-five percent of new energy in the country the year before was renewable, and every month, the cost seemed to come down. She could envision a day when electricity was clean, free, and everywhere. It felt like science fiction coming to life.

In fact — even though her to-be-read pile wrapped all the way around her room — she'd been slipping more climate fiction into her rotation, and some of them felt like a perfect mirror to her soul. Some were sad, but many were hopeful too, mourning our losses even as they envisioned another world, a needle we could thread to make ourselves anew. The other night, she'd read a story about three people transporting blueberries on a sailboat. When it was done, she'd shut her eyes, imagining her bakery was a little boat, her heat pump chugging like an engine as she floated through the night.

Even with the climate on her mind, though, she couldn't help but feel a spring in her step. Her non-date date had lifted her spirits, making her excited in a way she hadn't been in ages. Even if she was only making a new friend, meeting Arnold was something all her own, free of the crushing fear of failure everything else in her life revolved around. She'd even texted her high school friend — something she would have avoided like the plague before — giving her Arnold's contact for the animation club. Everything felt new now, brimming with possibility in a way it hadn't in ages.

Even better, Arnold would be coming back on Wednesday. They had little more than the *concept* of a plan, but he'd be stopping by again before close. She figured she could ply him with sweets and see where the night took them. Add that to today being her day off, and she had nothing to do but luxuriate in the feeling from the night before. That, and have a meeting with the butter man.

She always closed the bakery on Mondays, and while she tried to reserve part of the day for lying about and staring at the ceiling, she usually also tried to accomplish at least one horrible, looming task from her to-do list — combining it with a little adventure if she could. Today, her adventure was the butter man, yet another in a dozen (baker's dozen?) of failed attempts to generate buzz for the bakery.

The butter man — *legally* named Nick, which was boring compared to the more *butter-related* names out there — seemed to have none of her qualms about succeeding on social media. In addition to selling wholesale butter out of the French Market downtown, he also specialized in butter sculpture, something that had earned him some 300k followers.

Even if she could bake for hours, the moment Helen turned the camera on herself, she panicked, feeling instantly like a fraud. Unfortunately, that was the cost of doing business these days. And if she was going to fill people with magical baked goods, they'd need to *hear* about them first. When she DM'd the butter man on a whim, asking if she could use some of his sculptures in a round of bakes, he'd somehow miraculously said yes. Apparently, he liked her environmental bona fides, and they were going to collaborate on his fair trade coconut butter, giving her a chance to show off her electric oven.

The question now was what kind of shape to put the butter in. She'd been filling a notebook with suggestions, ranging anywhere from horoscopes to Pokémon. He would probably only be able to sculpt a handful of butters for her, but if she could use it to launch, say, a few dozen themed cupcakes or something, it should drum up at least *some* business. Then — and this was the part she couldn't tell Nick — she would bake feelings into them. That would really get things going — or scare away all her potential customers forever. Who knew? Life was risky!

She walked into the Rockwell station, the old wooden platform sitting at ground level and surrounded by homes and trees. Even for the late morning, there were dozens of people, the warm weather making them crawl outside like lizards on a rock. Having only lived in Chicago and New England, she didn't mind the cold, though it was always fun to see the excitement on everyone's faces when it got nice out. The Midwestern physique was suited to the cold, so even when it was only in the high sixties, there were already people in shorts and T-shirts.

She lacked the commitment to wear shorts so early in the year. Still, she *was* at least bringing her A-game. She'd thrown on an absurd-looking rain jacket from the eighties she'd found at Village Discount. It had hot pink sleeves and a bright green body, the entire thing covered in retro zig-zag shapes. It went with nothing, which, thankfully, meant it went with everything. Besides, once you started thrifting hard, you were allowed to free yourself from the strictures of caring about what anyone else thought. With waterproof gear poisoning the ground water with PFAS, she'd gladly run around town like a secondhand neon clown.

As the Brown Line finally pulled in — the train tracker never working this close to the end of the line — she couldn't help but look at all the other cars. Could Arnold be in one of them? She didn't know him well enough to know his school schedule or anything, but part of her still hoped she'd see his face peeking through the windows.

"Get a grip," she whispered to herself, ducking into the closest car. Wednesday was only two days away. She could go that long without seeing some boy who she most definitely would *not* be making her boyfriend — even if the foolish side of her secretly wanted to.

She grabbed one of the single seats by the window, pulling out her sketchbook. She wasn't much of an artist — unless you counted getting fifty-five layers in a croissant — but she still wanted something to work off of when she reached the butter man. Her favorite design so far was a cupcake with a giant turtle shell on its back, blue icing flowing off the side like water. She'd probably have to call it a "water turtle" for Pokémon copyright reasons, but her fellow nerds would know what it meant. She only had to hope Nick was similarly inclined. But what were butter men into? Maybe he'd only want to carve farm animals, forcing her to do a sort of zodiac situation.

She sighed, turning to a new page. She started doodling things she saw out the window — with a few random animals from the zodiac filling in the margins. The train snaked south, wrapping around buildings and over streets. The elevated train was one of the best parts of Chicago. She wouldn't be opposed to drawing underground subway rats, but they probably wouldn't be a good choice for baked goods.

She passed the Steppenwolf Theater, where the troupe staged mini-plays for the train on the parking deck in the summer. She sketched the Hancock Building, its two little antennas sticking out on top. Would Chicago landmarks look good in butter? Nick's followers were probably from everywhere, but she'd need to reach locals to sell her cupcakes. Baked goods could technically make good content, but her bakery was hardly equipped to start shipping cupcakes around the country.

But what feeling would she use? She closed her eyes, remembering the first time she went to the Hancock Building. Gran had taken her downtown for a girls' day, which usually meant tea at the Drake, followed by an American Girl doll. It gave her shivers to think about those ruddy-cheeked dolls filling her room, their 1800s backstories invariably tainted by tuberculosis or cholera. Still, she felt warm thinking of Gran, the red mittens she liked so much shoved in the older woman's hand. Everything felt so *big* when you were young, the old Water Tower like a princess castle with its brick spires rising in the air.

Helen licked her lips, suddenly tasting…*strawberries*. It was subtle, though, and cut with something. Balsamic? It would be an odd combination for a cupcake — better for a summer salad — but it could work. There were other flavors she was missing, but she intuitively knew the *feeling* she was tasting. It was about being small, about trusting an adult to take you somewhere magical.

A bit ironic perhaps, seeing as how a child would never willingly eat vinegar, but there was a richness to balsamic she must need to capture the feeling. After all, despite being young, there was something strangely eternal about being a kid, a ritual repeated over generations. Feeling that warm, that safe…it was a feeling she'd had all too rarely growing up, especially with—

She squeezed her eyes shut tighter. No. She would not be thinking about *that* — not today. The flavor vanished from her mouth, though she could still just about remember it. Once a flavor came to her, it usually never vanished completely from her mind. She jotted down the components she'd figured out thus far, calling it "doll flavor," which wasn't creepy at all. At least it was a start.

Finally, she reached the Loop, the trains starting their giant oval spin around downtown before shooting back out the way they came. Helen shoved her notebook in her bag, jumping off the train at the Wells stop, the early-1900s walls all painted green. She crossed the river, the wind whipping over the water as the water taxi floated past. Ahead, she could see Ogilvie Station, the long Metra trains flooding out from the tunnels like silver snakes.

Growing up, Gran had convinced her the building was named after Princess Alexandra Ogilvy, a cousin of the queen of England. How Gran knew something like that was anybody's guess, but when she'd moved back, Helen had looked it up. Apparently, it wasn't even the right Ogil-person, the station named after Governor Ogilvie, not Princess Ogilvy. The building looked fancy enough for a monarch, though, the old yellow brick out back topped with shining blue glass in front.

She wound around the side, coming up to where the French Market was shoved into the ground floor, its red canopies covering little tables full of people trying to take advantage of the weather. She stopped for a moment, taking a deep breath. For a second there, she'd been worried her feelings on the train would sweep her away. Grief could be like that, sneaking up only when your mind was quiet. But she *refused* to spend her day off sulking. The air was warm, the sky was bright, and it was time to meet the butter man.

Chapter Seventeen

Arnold reached the library just as the sun was setting behind the park. Most of the trees were still bare, but people were out with their dogs in the warmth, throwing tennis balls and frisbees. Sulzer, the giant regional library, was covered in skylights, and the glass picked up the setting sun, making the neighborhood glow orange. Why didn't he come here more? He thought that *every* time he saw the library, but it was still true. Even if he didn't have time for *fun* reading right now, he could still study here instead of in his apartment.

He'd spent his entire shift at the record store feeling like he was flying. The night before with Helen had gone shockingly well — especially when judged against his worst fears — and they'd be hanging out again in just two days. Maybe he was taking spring too literally, but it felt like he was *blossoming.* He'd gone from having no friends to having Lois, Helen, *and* a rowdy gang of spirits. If seeing spirits was madness, why had he ever wanted to be sane?

Of course, part of him was worried too. Ever since the incident out east, whenever something good happened, part of him felt like he was waiting for it to end. Last night, he'd had a movie to cover for him with Helen. But how long would it be until she realized he was boring and broken? And assuming he really was able to help Nüste — and Helen by proxy — could he really justify a place in her life after? He was a helper, a spirit gatherer, a...*placeholder.* Why would he ever think himself worthy of more?

He walked into the library, stopping at the front desk.

"Hey, I'm looking for the...animation club?"

"Oh, great," the kindly old librarian said. "There sure are a lot of you, huh?"

Arnold gulped, gripping his notebook a bit tighter. "A…lot of us?"

"New? Don't be scared. The others seemed perfectly nice. Upstairs on your left."

He nodded, forcing himself to smile. He couldn't run away now, not after Helen had gone to the trouble of introducing him to her friend Kylie, the head — owner? organizer? boss? — of the club. Besides, it was a Monday, so he was due at Ma's for dinner later. If he left now, he'd have two hours to fill and no excuse but to use them for homework.

He reached the second floor, where a bunch of glass study rooms were arranged in a long line opposite the stacks of books. One on the end was full of people, which probably meant it was the animation club. He started walking toward it, passing a row of computers, when he froze. On a chair next to him, there was a giant clump of grass swaying in an unseen wind. Was that…a spirit? Or a *bunch* of spirits? He shook his head, about to move on when he heard a giggle in his mind.

You can see us, can't you? a childlike voice asked. *We can tell.*

He shifted a bit closer to the chair. They were actually growing on *lots* of chairs, some tufts of grass even sticking out from under people's butts.

Yes, he thought.

The spirit giggled again. The sound seemed to be coming from all around him, echoing throughout the library as each blade of grass tittered in unison.

Sit if you like. When you sit, we exist.

Maybe in a bit, he thought carefully. *I have to go to that room over there. But…what are you?*

The spirit hummed as if thinking, sounding like a helicopter taking off as every blade of grass did so in unison.

We are a spirit of preference, of human opinion.

That was pretty much completely unhelpful, though he had begun — as far as such a thing was possible — to *almost* understand the way spirits thought.

Opinion about…chairs? Which chair we sit in?

Exactly! the spirits yelled, laughing again. *You're all so different. Some sit up front, some in back. We sprout where you think you'll be most comfortable.*

But he'd been riding transit since he started seeing spirits, hadn't he? Why hadn't he seen these before? Or was he simply becoming more sensitive? Nüste *had* said his third eye would keep opening, but did that mean even more spirits were out there waiting for him? He hadn't noticed these grass spirits on the train that morning, though he'd obviously been thinking about something — or someone — else.

I didn't see many on the train today. Do you not grow there?

We grow everywhere, the spirit thought as if it were obvious. *But sometimes thicker, yes, yes. Look in human homes. A dining table, a sofa… Where the opinion is stronger, we grow bigger. Oh, and when there is a favorite — incredible!*

He pictured his own parents' favorite chairs. Flanking the TV, Ma's was an old plaid recliner, while dad had picked up a used La-Z-Boy he was obsessed with, the tan leather slowly growing blue beneath his jeans. Would those be covered in grass when he visited for dinner?

Part of him wanted to reach out and pluck one, but would this even be a good spirit to take to Helen's? Having a favorite chair *was* comforting in a way, but they were pretty creepy too. Helen wouldn't know the difference, but he couldn't quite shake his fear of Nüste telling him off. He had plenty of time until they hung out Wednesday, though. If these...*things* really were growing everywhere, he could always pick one later.

Do you...travel?

With you? the grass spirit chittered. *We sense your anchor. So strong. You pluck, we come. We grow bigger if you let us.*

He imagined putting one on his shoulder like the other spirits only spreading like wildfire, covering his back until he couldn't move.

Uh, maybe next time, he thought. *But thank you. It's...good to know. I'll see you around.*

Before he could see anything else, Arnold marched into the study room, a sign reading "Animation Club" taped to the door.

"Uh...hey," he said as everyone looked up from laptops and notebooks. There were a dozen people, a hodgepodge of ages.

A woman in a yellow sweater smiled at him. "You Arnold? I'm Kylie, Helen's friend."

"Oh, yeah," he said, nodding. "Thanks for having me."

"Hey, Arnold!" a few people yelled, making him smile. It was impossible to be around animators without someone linking him to the show. Luckily, it was one of the best shows ever made, so he always took it as a compliment.

"Grab a seat," Kylie said. "We can start with intros."

Arnold took one of the open chairs, trying to ignore the spiritual grass growing on it. One by one, the others introduced themselves, sharing what they were working on. It felt like being at RISD again, the sheer volume of creativity overwhelming. There were pirate swordfights being animated in Adobe, a 3-D squid made in Maia. There were even lots of colored pencils and paint — which made him feel less embarrassed about only bringing a notebook. Finally, the circle came around to him.

"And what are you working on tonight, Arnold?"

"I just thought I'd do some sketching, I guess. It's...been a while."

"No shame in that! Now, whose turn was it on the playlist?"

A great chorus of arguments broke out at that. Apparently, they picked the music in ten-minute increments, though the system for who picked and when was completely incomprehensible to him. In the end, a guy named Roger won, and he put on some Bossa nova through a Bluetooth speaker in the middle of the table. Part of him was worried a librarian would yell at them, but it really wasn't all that loud with the door shut.

Arnold opened his notebook, quickly flipping past the pages of work he'd abandoned back in Rhode Island. He couldn't bring himself to tear the pages out, but he didn't want to look at them, either. The version of himself who'd been working on those was gone. But what should he replace them with? He stared at the blank page in front of him for a long time, flipping his pencil back and forth between his fingers. At school, he'd been really into caricatures, doing funny versions of teachers, politicians, whoever. It felt a little silly now, though. Who really knew him well enough to care?

In the end, he just started making shapes, dragging his pencil in a wide circle. Then he made smaller ones, connecting them like he might have back in school, movable shapes he could animate. Before he realized it, he was drawing Nüste. He pictured the little mushroom spirit in his mind, trying to remember how he moved. Mostly, Nüste just…bounced, right? Arnold typically only saw him yelling through the window, but he could imagine how a mushroom with no arms got around. He started again, drawing the next gesture.

"That's really cool," the woman next to him — Beth? — said, pointing at his notebook.

"Oh…thanks. Just did the first thing that came to mind."

"Well, interesting mind you got there," she said, chuckling. "I'm making a platypus army."

She turned her computer toward him, showing what was indeed an army of…platypi? platypuses?…storming a beach.

"This is amazing," he said, earning a smile from Beth before she went back to work.

It's platypuses, the grass spirit said beneath him. *It's Greek not Latin. Platys for flat and pous for foot.*

Arnold cocked his head, his pencil hovering above the page.

How do you know that? Do…platypuses have a preference for where they sit?

The grass chittered, a chorus of laughter rising throughout the library again.

No! But we know things… many things.

That wasn't entirely reassuring. Were grass spirits just constantly eavesdropping on humans, making their way through a world of chairs to overhear…the correct pluralization of platypus? He glanced at Beth's computer. Did he really have an interesting mind? Or was he losing it, taking grammar lessons from a patch of grass? Would she — or anyone in the animation club — be okay with the fact that his fanciful "drawings" were real spirits? Maybe they *would*. After all, Helen had liked him enough to connect him with Kylie.

He took a deep breath, managing to smile. He started drawing again, making the next frame of Nüste's body. He would keep it simple for now, but it felt *good* to draw again. Even if he was drawing a wild little mushroom man, he felt freer than he had in a long time.

———

By the time he got to his parents' house, Arnold could see them through the window, already setting the table for dinner. He'd stayed late, chatting with the other animators until he'd finally noticed the clock, his eyes jumping out of his head. He hadn't even had time to walk. He'd jumped on an electric scooter, zipping through the back alleys and flying over speed bumps until he landed in their front yard. He hid the scooter behind some bushes, rushing up the steps.

"I'm here!" he called, entering through the back door that was always open. "Sorry!"

"Arn," Ma said, popping her head out from the dining room, a concerned frown on her face. "What happened? I was beginning to worry."

He smiled, ignoring the twinge in the stomach he felt every time Ma looked at him like an egg about to crack. *She loves you*, he reminded himself. It was Ma who came to Rhode Island to get him, Ma who had sacrificed so much to help him start over in Chicago. He just…wished she could see the other parts of him as well.

"I had my study group," he said, dropping the canned lie like it was nothing. "From school."

He always had a few lies handy for his parents, and he'd been slowly building up a fake study group in their minds, name-dropping the same few kids from his class as if they were friends. It was nothing nefarious; he just knew what Ma expected, and he rushed to give it to her. She cared for him fiercely, but there was only one way to be with Ma.

In high school, he'd had his performance down perfectly. It was only after his incident that the lifelong facade came crashing down, forcing him to constantly reassure her that he was *okay*. But he had friends now, didn't he? He was getting better. It didn't feel like as much of a lie anymore.

"Oh, good," Ma said, finally smiling. "Well, make sure you study hard. I know those quizzes are tough."

Arnold gulped, accepting the container of rice Ma gave him to carry from the kitchen. His Psych 203 class was structured as a series of pop quizzes, which counted for a massive third of his grade. So far, since he always did his reading, it hadn't been *too* difficult. But as he tried to picture his textbook back at his apartment, he genuinely couldn't remember how much of the reading he'd done lately. To say he'd been *distracted* would be a massive understatement.

As if on cue, one of his many tiny distractions appeared. Coming around the corner of the dining room, he found the chairs covered in preference grass, the spirits grown tall from the many years of assigned seating at their family dinners.

Welcome back! the grass laughed in unison. *We've been waiting for you.*

Chapter Eighteen

Helen had woken up on Wednesday with another feeling in her mind. Like an alarm clock worming its way into your sleep, she had dreamt it first. But as she opened her eyes to a cloudy Wednesday morning, she found the flavor still on her tongue. It was a remembered flavor, a memory of the first cookies she'd ever baked with Gran. Could people even remember flavors from that long ago? Maybe she'd made it up, but she found she still believed, sitting up and reaching for her phone so she could jot it down. Her notes app was getting full of these strange new recipes, but the more she focused on them, the more she seemed to come up with.

In this memory, she'd been six, the first summer she lived in this apartment. Dad had probably been there, but she couldn't place him. In fact, most of her memories of him were gone, locked up where they belonged. The only thing she could remember about him was the time he took her to a White Sox game, his black-and-white jacket stitched with a giant *Sox* emblem. She brushed the ghost of him away, focusing on the happier memories of Gran.

It had to have been summer, when she'd spend every day with Gran from sunup to sundown, following her around the house and down into the bakery. Gran had been in the spoon-licking generation, and before Helen was big enough to help, she could still lick the batter from the utensils — salmonella be damned.

On that particular day, though, she'd been deemed big enough — or tall enough, perhaps — to bake. It had felt like Christmas, like unwrapping a gift she'd waited for her whole life. Days like that had put the dream in her, the dream that she could be more like Gran, that she could run the bakery someday. Even if the road between then and now had been paved with tears, it had begun with smiles. It had begun with *baking*.

"Thees cookie ees important," Gran said, never quite shaking her accent, despite all her decades in Chicago. "Ees first cookie *my* Gran taught *me*, yes?"

She told the story of her village, a paradise, rolling green hills and a river behind their house, the sound of running water like a constant lullaby. But these cookies had a *meaning*. They were baked before the first full moon of spring, to protect the fields from *demons*. Half would be eaten by the family, but the rest would be crushed and scattered in the fields, filling the bellies of crows who would keep their people safe.

"Beeg red eyes," Gran said, describing the demons as she urged Helen to pour in the ingredients. "Claws as long as your hair."

She tugged on Helen's ponytail, making her laugh.

"Good, yes? Laugh, little one! Demons hate happy."

The recipe called for oats and winter wheat, the remnants of the last harvest used to protect the next one. It was joined by honey and nuts before all of it was mixed in with nutmeg and brown sugar. She could still remember the pungent nutmeg wafting from the jar, making her wrinkle her little nose.

"Why do we use this?" Helen asked. "Does this scare demons too?"

"No, child. Nutmeg was eexpensive when I was bebby. It mean hope harvest weel be good enough to buy again. Hope makes us laugh, laugh to spite the demon."

"But they're just cookies."

"Nothing ees just cookies," Gran said, getting serious. She'd leaned down, meeting Helen's eyes. "You know where from demons come?"

Helen shook her head, imagining a demon climbing through her window. Thankfully, Gran never minded when Helen climbed into her big, fluffy bed at night, letting her cuddle when she had bad dreams.

"Demons is men. Men who lose hope, forget joy. Nothing — what is your English word — *freevolous* about joy, so nothing *freevolous* about cookies."

That had stayed with her. Despite Gran dying, despite the years they'd been forced to live apart, she still thought about it. During culinary school, she'd even had it tattooed on her arm, the word for demon in Gran's language wrapped up in the words for hope and joy. After all, in their age of unfettered capitalism, wasn't there something...*rebellious* about sweets? In a world that wanted everyone to be a number on a spreadsheet, here was an *indulgence*, a battle cry for joy.

Maybe baking wouldn't change the world on its *own*, but what could? Like it said in *Oathbringer*, the world was a rock rolling down a hill, and the truly wise knew they could only nudge it to the side. Everyone had to change the world *together*, and if all Helen did was fuel the revolution with cookies, she'd still be happy. She could do her part — electrifying, using fair trade ingredients — but in the end, her contribution was just that, a tiny piece of the whole.

She got up, stumbling toward the kitchen. Maybe she should have been normal for once — given herself a leisurely morning, drunk a coffee — but there were battles to be won, and she'd be waging them with nutmeg.

———

Nüste woke to the sound of chatter. Spirits didn't *technically* need to sleep, but after two days of serving his guests, he'd needed a break. So, he'd shut his nonexistent eyes, tapped into the spirit of moonlight, and listened to her song until he forgot where he was. Besides, it wasn't like Helen would be baking in her sleep, so why not get a little shut-eye at night? He looked up toward the ceiling. There, floating among the rafters, were swirling pools of green and beige, the spirits having shed enough of themselves to fill the attic with their emotions.

It would probably take a while for Helen to notice, of course. Even sensitive humans like her had to absorb foreign emotions slowly, like a virus working its way past the immune system. It would probably be another day or two before—

Nutmeg.

Nüste sat up, the eyes of the moss and bagel spirits swiveling toward him. He sighed, part of him having hoped they'd see their way out — which was wishful thinking, obviously. Spirits weren't like humans. They had nowhere to be and weren't likely to move on without some light exorcism.

"Is she baking?" he asked them, ignoring his annoyance. He had to hang on to his excitement. If she was using the feelings from his cafe in her bakery, it meant this was all beginning to work. It meant he'd soon be *free*.

"Baking?" the moss spirit asked — as if he'd said a word from Mars. If only Nüste had appeared on Mars this time… He'd been all over the solar system, and he much preferred the new beginnings of subterranean single-celled bacteria to this maddening nonsense.

"Yes, baking. The *girl*. Can you tell what she's doing?"

The bagel snorted. "I'd hardly call it baking. She hasn't even boiled it first."

"Well, she's not making *bagels*," Nüste said, ignoring them as he moved toward the center of the attic. Standing directly under the pool of emotions, he could sense a sort of conduit, a vein of feeling running from above to below. That had to be Helen.

Keeping going, girl, he thought, urging her on with all his might. *Don't give up now.*

And don't you give up either, he thought to himself. This was *working*. He just had to see it through. He sucked in a deep, lung-less breath, putting on his happy host face.

"Apologies for my earlier demeanor," he said, smiling as if he had those obsequious little lips humans liked so much. "But, my dear customers, I'm afraid it's time to clear your tables. I'm expecting a fresh batch of friends tonight, and I'm afraid I'll need ample time to clean."

Neither of them moved. In fact, the moss spirit's eye had rolled back into her gelatinous head, leaving a lump of…*something* in her place. Well, they were about to see just how many new beginnings a spirit like him could conjure —

first of which would be throwing these spirits out on their ears. It might not help his Yelp reviews, but he had a girl to save.

Chapter Nineteen

"Well, that's one idea gone," Arnold said to himself, squinting at the sky.

Massive gray clouds drifted in from the horizon, their bottoms heavy with a future storm. He traced the veins of blue through the clouds, always reminded of his first oil painting class. Clouds were so much more complicated than they seemed, needing hundreds of little brush strokes to convey the whorls of precipitation.

He shook his head, looking away. There had been a gap in the clouds earlier, and he'd seen…*something* up there. It had been like a ring in the sky, a shimmering silver circle floating in the air. It had looked incredibly high up, like a plane you spotted only by its trail of clouds, hazy as it glided through the stratosphere. It had seemed to *attract* all the tiny blue souls of people floating ever higher. Like it was some kind of *heaven*.

Growing up, he'd found the thought of heaven terrifying. Even though they sold it to you as a straightforward thing — puffy white clouds, people in robes, no more tears — conceptually it had never quite added up for him. After all, how was a human mind supposed to wrap itself around eternity anyway? Setting aside the ridiculous medieval scare tactics surrounding hell, even going to heaven was scary in its own right. The lines of "Amazing Grace," "when we've been here ten thousand years," had been enough to give him chills.

Thankfully, his conception of God had expanded, freeing him from the rigidity he grew up with. Because, if he was honest, everything they'd taught in kids' church was basically just a hyperbolic blend of folklore and *Paradise Lost.* What he'd finally realized was that heaven had to be completely different from what he knew. It had to be like the other side of a black hole, freeing you from time all together — rather than simply giving you too much of it.

Still, he hardly had time to think of any of that now. He was on his way to Helen's — and desperately trying to think of cool ideas for their "hang." He'd originally hoped to take her kayaking on the North Branch of the river. Just down the block, Horner Park turned what was basically a stinky canal into a lush paradise, flanked by reeds and filled with turtles and muskrats patrolling the water. Unfortunately, it seemed the weather had other plans. The warmth of the past few days had lulled him into forgetting what March was really like in Chicago.

He walked toward the train, running through his backup ideas. The problem wasn't thinking of other things to do in a giant city, it was thinking of something that wasn't horribly nerdy. They could see a black-and-white movie at the Music Box — which, despite *seeming* like awkward cinephile fare, at least promised the best popcorn in Chicago. They could also see the new exhibit at the MCA, an entire wing of abstract paintings about food. But would all these food ideas feel reductive and pandering? Helen wasn't *just* a baker. She was…well, *amazing.*

Helen *was* still new to Chicago, though — or newly returned, anyway — so taking her to new places would be nice, whether they were food-themed or not, right? He'd noticed her massive book collection, so there were always book shops to try. He could also simply be trying too hard. After all, this wasn't a date — even if his second official hang with Helen *felt* high-stakes. In the end, the only thing he could do was present Helen with some choices and allow himself to be tugged along in her effervescent wake.

Heehee, the spirit on his shoulder chuckled. *We enjoy this.*

There was also the tagalong he had to drop off. Between work, school, and the drawing he couldn't seem to stop doing, he'd run out of time to find spirits for Nüste. In the end, he'd gathered a bunch of the grass spirits from his parents' house, though it was starting to seem like a mistake. He'd taken a single frond from his dad's favorite chair, and now there were *three*. Would Nüste be mad? He didn't want to start a grass infestation in Helen's attic, but how were they supposed to run a spirit cafe with the little mushroom being so picky all the time?

Arnold got on the train, glancing down at his outfit as he sat. Was his shirt cool enough? It was vintage, an old plaid button-down with the original mother of pearl buttons. It seemed like the kind of thing Helen might like with all her thrifting, though he also needed it to be casual. It needed to say, "this is a hang, and I am *not* being weird about it." Then again, it now had *five* grass fronds growing from it, which was hardly "casual."

We see you chose this seat, the blades of grass all said in unison. *Its flavor bears a small preference. Delicious!*

Did he prefer this seat? He'd picked one of the singles again, though everyone did that when they were available, didn't they?

Uh…thanks, he thought in return. *I'm glad you like it.*

By the time Arnold arrived, he was thanking his lucky stars Helen's was only a few stops from his place. There were ten grass fronds on his shoulder, and they were starting to seed some of the chairs around him, growing as new riders joined at every stop. As they came into Rockwell, he waited until the last second, jumping out as the doors closed, so more couldn't follow after him.

As he came out onto the street, he could see Nüste in the window already. The little mushroom spirit clearly had some ability to sense Arnold from a distance, always poking up his little head before he reached out with his mind. But how far could such a power reach? He suddenly felt a chill, imagining Nüste watching over his shoulder at every turn. It was bad enough having spirits hiding around every corner without one watching on spirit CCTV.

Wait, wait, wait! Nüste yelled, waving with both arms. *You brought seat spirits? Do you have any idea how hard those are gonna be to get rid of?*

Beggars can't be choosers, Arnold thought, waiting for a car to pass before he jogged across the street. *These aren't a bad feeling, though, right? I think Helen would like a comfortable chair.*

Fine, Nüste thought with a huff. *But if you did your job, I wouldn't have just these for customers.*

I just brought you two the other day! If you want me to keep—

Alright, kid, relax, Nüste interrupted. *Thanks for the spirits. I'm sure I'll manage. Since when did you get so testy?*

This is harder than it looks! Arnold thought. He paused just out of view of the bakery window. *I'm doing my best.*

We like this place, the grass spirits chittered. *Strong opinions here; much to eat. We hunger.*

Absolutely spine-chilling, Nüste thought, sighing. *You lot, make your way up here. Only one seat per frond, though, I got a cafe to run! If you start spreading, you'd better believe I'll get my hedge trimmers out.*

The grass spirits giggled again, sucking down into Arnold's shoulder like a snake retreating into a hole. As they did, he felt their weight just…*disappear*, their laughter suddenly filtering down from the attic.

You better pray this does the girl some good, Nüste thought, seeming to point right at Arnold despite a lack of hands. *I can always find someone else, you know.*

Somehow, Arnold doubted that. He'd never been anyone's first pick for anything, and for all of Nüste's swagger, there was a sort of…*desperation* about the little mushroom in Helen's attic.

Yeah, yeah, Arnold said, finally heading for the door. *I'll see you soon.*

As the bell rang above the door, he found Helen head-down over a bunch of cookies. Like some sort of kitchen Guanyin, she always looked the part of a goddess, her thousand arms full of tiny baked-good mercies. She looked up from her icing, her eyes going wide.

"Is it time already?" she asked, pushing the hair out of her face with her wrist. "It's the only thing I've thought about all day, and still the time got away from me."

All she'd been thinking about? While that single sentence made it feel like a hundred balloons had popped in his chest, he tried not to make too much of it. He sat at one of the open tables, ignoring how sweaty his palms were.

"No rush," he said. "What are you working on?"

"A new cookie recipe, which you'll obviously be tasting, my dear, dear guinea pig."

She slammed about the kitchen for another minute before throwing off her apron and coming around the side, a plate in hand. She placed it in front of him before locking the door and flipping the *open* sign to *closed.*

"I don't know why I'm like this," she said, sitting across from him as she tapped the side of her head. "When I'm baking, there's nothing but a dial tone in here."

"The soul of an artist," Arnold said, picking up the cookie. He held it delicately like a treasure, which in many ways, it was. She'd done the icing to look like a pot of gold, with little gold coins brimming from a glossy black base. It *was* almost St. Patrick's Day, when the city would explode into a mass of drunken parades.

"What's the secret feeling this time?" he asked.

Helen looked at him with an intensity he wasn't used to. "Did you *really* taste prom the other night? I know my flavors are a little weird…"

"They're lovely," he said firmly, taking a bite. "And I really did. I don't know how you do it, but it tasted like—"

A memory suddenly pushed into his mind. It was Christmas. He wasn't sure what year, but there were presents under the tree and he was small. He found himself sizing up the boxes, wondering what was inside. Most of them were labeled "From Ma." Even when she'd pretended Santa was real, she'd never been able to accept some random old man taking credit for all her hard work. Still, for however hard she pushed him during the year, Ma loved Christmas, loved making his tiny wishes come true.

"I'm getting…nutmeg," Arnold said, opening his eyes to find Helen still watching him. "It's like Christmas, but not a Christmas cookie. Like…*Christmas Christmas* — the feeling, the holiday."

He thought of the spirits he'd dropped off to the cafe before, Poppyseed and Clara's Dream. Were they already influencing Helen's bakes? They were both about longing, in a way, but did that combine to make Christmas? Or was that something special added by Helen herself? He could never ask her out loud — not without her thinking him insane. Still, if it meant the spirits were working, if it meant he was really *helping*…

"That's what I was going for," she said, smiling. "You have *excellent* taste buds. You sure you didn't pick the wrong art form?"

He snorted, shaking his head. "If my life is any indication, I'm pretty positive

I've picked the wrong *everything*. Other than this cookie and hanging out with you, of course."

"Hardly," she said, taking the plate to the kitchen as he popped the rest of the cookie in his mouth. "I'll have you know I've watched your videos at least a dozen times. They're really great."

"Nah, they're not, it's—"

"Hey," she said turning back, hands on her hips as she interrupted him. "They're *really* good. Don't get all humble on me now. What would you do if I said my cookies were disgusting?"

"Well, I mean, baking is definitely an art form, but like…*objectively*, they're mouth-watering. It's pretty hard to argue with."

"Maybe my mouth watered while I was watching your animations. What then?"

"Then…thank you?" he said, laughing. "Actually, I genuinely need to thank you. I went to Kylie's animation club, and I've been drawing every day since. It's been… I don't know, kind of a miracle, actually."

"Oh, I'm so glad!" Helen said from behind the counter. "What have you been drawing? Better not be drawing me like one of your French girls."

He felt his chest flush with heat. Even if she was joking, the *thought* of it… Still, it was better than explaining that he was drawing the *spirits* hiding in her attic.

"You caught me," he said, joining her on the other side of the counter. "If you have the Heart of the Ocean from *Titanic*, though, we should probably talk about how you're laundering all that money."

"Trust me," she said as she washed some dishes, "you can hide millions in a rinky-dink bakery. The butter costs alone…"

He stared down at all the baked goods in the case. It was like looking at a pile of treasure.

"Hey, what's that?" he asked, pointing at one in the back. It looked like a cross between a Squirtle and a croissant, the lacquered brown shell giving way to a curly blue tail.

"A 'promotional experiment,'" she said with air quotes, squatting down so she was eye level with the bottom row of treats. She pulled it out, handing it to him. "I'm working with a butter guy on weird-shaped butter. He has a big following, so hopefully people will come to eat the things with his butter in it. I don't know, it's silly."

"It's a mouth-watering art form, remember?" Arnold said, giving her a look before she became as self-deprecating as he was. He held it up to the light. "I think it's great. It's Squirtle, right? Also — you have a butter guy?"

"Every baker has a butter guy," she said, grinning as she took back the pastry. "It's the first thing they ask on your culinary school applications. But enough about that, what are we doing today?"

Arnold gulped. This was the moment of truth, the moment when her eyes would either light up or look crestfallen at his awful ideas.

"Well…I thought of some options. It's not nice enough for kayaking, but I do have some backups."

"Adventurous," she said, nodding, "I like it. What else you got?"

He outlined the other options, basically giving a dissertation on why he'd picked each one. Luckily — and in step with the rest of her perfect personality — she was spontaneous enough to avoid getting bogged down by the hundreds of contingencies he'd anxiously planned for.

"Movie, definitely," she said. "I gotta up my cinema game if I'm gonna be hanging around with Mr. Animation."

"Is Mr. Animation a compliment?"

"It is," she said, winking.

Helen went around the corner behind the oven, rooting around by the freezers. She reappeared, a ridiculously cool vintage windbreaker in hand.

"And we're off!" she said, heading for the exit.

As they stepped onto the sidewalk, Helen locking the door behind them, Arnold could hear Nüste shouting in his mind.

No, no, I said one chair each! One chair!

Sorry, Arnold thought to him. Still, it was hard to feel *too* bad when there was a goddess in front of him on the sidewalk. He just had to hope her house wasn't covered in grass when they got back…

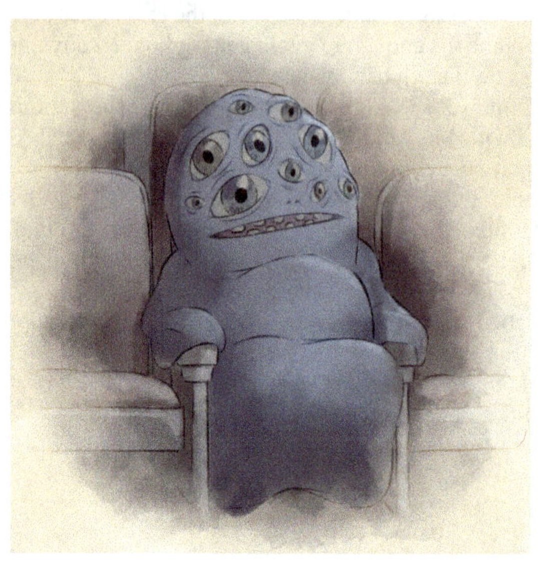

Chapter Twenty

Helen followed Arnold out of the Southport Brown Line stop, hoping he wouldn't go headlong down the stairs as he tried to keep the conversation going backward. Still, she appreciated his hustle. He worked at conversation like she would kneading dough. Not in an *annoying* way. In an…*earnest* way. He was incredibly easy to talk to, and he actually listened to her — which she couldn't say for the last five or six dozen men she'd talked to. He took in every word she said like it was flour, baking it in his little brain-oven before giving it back to her with a refreshing perspective.

"But I really do agree. The like…physics of that first book are wild, the way the planes flip and everything. Ugh, so good."

They'd started talking sci-fi and fantasy, and they were now trading opinions on the Cytoverse. It probably helped that she was spending time with someone — in an entirely *non-date* fashion — who actually shared some of her interests. She'd been burnt by nerds before — any man was capable of being a dick. But in her mind, there were nerds and there were *nerds*, men who tried to break your Dragon Ball scouter with how "smart" they were. In the end, the old adage held true — only *interested* people were interesting, and Arnold genuinely cared about what she had to say.

"Where on earth have you brought me?" she asked, stepping through the gate and onto the street.

She hadn't had much of a chance to venture down to Southport, but it seemed like a dangerous place indeed. Right by the train stop, there was a Jeni's, the smell of waffle cones shimmering in the air. It was a bit more corporate than she liked — Lincoln Square, after all, only had a single Starbucks that had managed to sneak into their mom-and-pop paradise. Still, there was a charm to having all the random chains you remembered from childhood. She didn't have to buy anything to spend an hour in a Lush, smelling bath bombs.

"The smell?" he asked, joining her as she cupped her hands over the window at Jeni's, staring at the double rows of ice cream. "Just wait until you smell the popcorn."

"Yes," she said, closing her eyes as she took a deep breath. "Popcorn. Don't let me forget."

"I swear this is as bad as it gets. It's not like they have cookies at the Paper Source."

Eventually, they escaped the clutches of their corporate overlords, crossing over Addison, where at least there was a local taco joint with a bright pink sign. It had to hide behind a massive Jewel-Osco, but you couldn't have everything in life. Thankfully, the theater was ahead, *The Music Box* in bright red neon in front of a facade that looked like a cathedral — and perhaps it was, though one where people worshipped movies.

"You done good, kid," she said to Arnold, following him across the street.

"I hope so. I'll grab tickets?" he asked, pointing at the box office.

That was an awfully date-like behavior, and certainly not one she needed him to make a habit of.

"We can go Dutch; I'm a big girl. Or I can get the popcorn?"

"Oh, yeah, sure," he said, waving his hands in apology. "I swear it's not a creepy dude thing. I would've paid with a guy friend too. It's like… I guess the movie feels like my fault? Like it was my idea, so I should pay. And then if you don't like the movie, it's better if I paid, you know? Like… I'm sorry."

She started laughing. Earnest was *definitely* the right word. At least he was cute when he squirmed.

"Well, first of all, going to a lovely movie at a lovely theater is not anyone's *fault.* But since you're such a gentleman about it — *thank you* for the tickets. I will definitely go in and get the popcorn. Anything else? You a candy guy?"

They briefly debated the merits of Reese's versus Sno-Caps before she went inside. Although, she didn't make it far into the lobby before it hit her. The *smell!* He was right. It was like a hurricane made of butter — *real* butter — pulling up a thousand memories of movies with Gran when she was a girl. Never mind the dope mosaic floor tiles and the scrollwork on the wood; she was in heaven.

Suppose she made a Music Box popcorn-butter croissant instead? Would people go for that? She waited in line, calculating how many tons of popcorn and candy she could buy that instant without bankrupting the bakery. Heaven indeed.

———

Arnold — his arms laden with an aggressive amount of popcorn — followed Helen into the theater, where the organist was setting up. Music Box did a silent film with the organ once a month — which was a draw in and of itself — but he'd been so focused on getting Helen to try their popcorn, he hadn't really even thought about the movie. Date or not, was it smart to take a new friend to *Nosferatu*? Would she like it? Was 1922 *too* vintage? Would it remind her that she was hanging out with a guy who basically *looked* like a vampire with his weird ears and buck teeth? There was a cutout of the creature near the organ, his face perpetually surprised despite centuries of bloodthirsty plotting.

"Where do you want to sit?" Helen asked, interrupting his terrified spiraling.

"Oh, anywhere," he said, praying he wouldn't attract more grass spirits. Helen's preference could probably attract them too, though she seemed whimsical enough to not have any firm opinions on movie seating — especially for a theater she'd never been to. Luckily, the Music Box also defied the current standards of moviegoing stadium seating, the old cinema chairs divided into three columns.

"Hmmm…there!" she said, pointing at the inner section.

"Perf—" he started to say before he stopped. Would declaring the seats "perfect" attract the grass anyway? "Er…fine by me."

"Hey, you're the movie buff," she said, chuckling as she nudged him with her elbow — which was no easy feat with her own hands full of snacks.

As they wound around the back, he noticed something out of the corner of his eye, a spirit hovering above him. He spared a glance for the ceiling, where a dark blue blob was waiting in the darkness above the projector. He didn't dare look closer — he could hardly manage the conversation with Helen as it was — but it seemed to have *hundreds* of eyes. A…cinema spirit, perhaps?

"Have you seen this one before?" he asked, his voice suddenly hoarse.

"Oh, yeah," she said, beaming as she looked over her shoulder at him. "I…went through a vampire phase."

"Happens to the best of us," he said, laughing. "How about the Dave Eggers one?"

"Obviously! I mean…it *is* the best Christmas movie since *Die Hard*."

Somehow, they got situated despite their mountain of concessions. Thankfully, the movie started not long after, the lights dimming to hide the spirit behind him. For all he knew, there could be dozens of them in a place this old, but all he had to do was stare at a screen. Well, *that*, and act normal for an hour and a half. And not eat weird. Or yawn, or fart, or any other embarrassing thing while he was sitting next to the coolest person in Chicago.

"Alright," Helen whispered, an ad for a film festival showing on the screen. "Do you trust me to make the magic happen?"

He nodded, and she cracked her knuckles, going to work on their little pile of salt and sugar. She started opening candy packages, handing him things as she dug a hole in the popcorn. She poured candy into the center before shaking the bag, mixing everything to perfection. As she opened it, he half-expected a spirit to appear, summoned by her new creation.

"Voila," she said, offering him the first bite.

"It's…an honor," he said, taking what he hoped was a normal handful — respectful of her art from without selfishly hogging too much for himself. And before long — the Music Box sparing them the twenty-minute trailer apocalypse of a corporate theater — the title card lit the screen in blue, the organ wailing away.

He did his best to watch the movie, but sitting there in the dark, it was hard not to think about Helen. Even the way she ate popcorn was beautiful somehow, taking these giant scoops she then managed to get in her mouth without spilling. There was something…*passionate* in the way she ate popcorn, like an artist revealing their essence through their brushstrokes.

Then there was the armrest. Even with no ill intent — and a burning desire not to be creepy — it was a loaded piece of furniture. How many dates had he been on in high school where he'd stared at it out of the corner of his eye, waiting for some signal he could reach out with his pinky? Hideous, blood-sucking monster beside, this suddenly felt like a terrible idea for a friend-hang. If they'd been at the museum, he could have kept his distance, pointing at the art from ten feet away, too far to see her elegantly destroy her popcorn.

The floor seemed to ripple beneath him, as if it were suddenly made of water. He tried to avoid looking down, but he saw a spirit pass beneath their feet, its skin a mottled pink, a row of eyes looking up at him. He tightened his grip on the chair, staring intently at the screen. Had he attracted this creature with his thoughts about holding Helen's hand? Or was it some kind of sign he was *supposed* to think about it?

That was a terrible line of thinking. He couldn't start using every apparition to justify whatever he secretly wanted in his heart — especially knowing how little he deserved someone like Helen. At some point, with your life in shambles and your brain full of phantoms, you had to admit you weren't exactly a *catch*.

Still — aside from his own wayward romantic ambitions — it *was* an important question, wasn't it? A chicken-or-egg for the spiritual realm. Were spirits simply attracted to things, as Nüste seemed to imply, or — in the case of Helen's seemingly magical bakes — were they *causing* the thing? Perhaps the type of spirit mattered? The pure-emotion spirits were clearly different than the blob spirits, popping up and fading as quickly as the feelings themselves.

He'd read that in the Talmud, every blade of grass has an angel standing over it, urging it to grow. That would be an argument for the latter, that spirits were somehow *causal* in the human realm, pushing them toward outcomes on the pinwheel of cosmic possibility. Or something like that. Actually, it made him wonder about every myth and tale from history. Had people seen spirits like he did in the past? Or were they seeing something else? And what about vampires, for that matter? He'd heard the stories about medieval illness and all of that, but was there a spirit attracted to stories like that, some horror spirit feeding off their fear?

The organ cried out again, pulling his attention back to the screen. Nosferatu had appeared, his inhuman ears shining in the darkness. Maybe it was better to pay attention to the movie, especially if it helped him avoid eye contact with the…*thing* beneath their feet. He put his hand on his lap, getting it away from the shared airspace between himself and Helen. He was lucky to be here — *overjoyed* even — but it seemed he had a long night ahead of him. Seeing spirits clearly wouldn't make hanging out in public easy, especially if he was meant to act like a normal person.

This better work, Nüste, he thought, careful not to speak it in his mind, lest another spirit hear. He tossed some popcorn in his mouth, closing his eyes. *This had better work.*

Chapter Twenty-one

Helen glanced at Arnold, noticing his hands had retreated to his lap. She'd been right on the verge of grabbing one, some strange nostalgia about being in a movie theater with a cute guy nearly hijacking her brain.

Stop being impulsive, she thought, slowly letting out a sigh. Arnold wasn't a batch of brownies. If she made the wrong move, she wouldn't be able to take it back, and she'd have ruined her first new friendship in Chicago. Still…he *did* look cute sitting there, glowing in the light from the screen.

You're a monster, she thought, taking a sip of her drink. She knew she was wildly unfit to date. And yet, here she was ready to throw caution to the wind. It was like getting in a car without knowing how to drive. Maybe she'd make it down the block, but she'd cause a fiery crash eventually, wouldn't she? She tried to think again of what her last partner had told her before she left Boston.

"There isn't room for me. It's just you and whatever it is you won't let go of."

It had become a sort of mantra for her, though she wasn't entirely sure what to do with it anymore. In the beginning, it had been enough to swear off dating. But now? Was she *really* holding on to something so tightly there wasn't room for someone else? She had her own dreams, true, but the bakery was more or less on its way. Was it her childhood? Everyone had things they'd rather forget, but what did that have to do with romance?

Still, she had to admit there had been a *distance* in all her relationships, whether she created it on purpose or not. She liked to think she was at least *kind* to the people she dated. She usually left them off better than she'd found them, giving them a safe enough place to work through their own stuff. But had she ever really let them in? In the end, she'd always found a reason not to. *She was leaving town. They didn't want the same things. They weren't right for each other.* They were the kind of euphemisms that hid a lot of sins, but they felt true too.

After all, how else were you meant to head off disaster? She hardly remembered her parents' divorce, but she'd spent an entire lifetime dealing with the fallout from it. Hadn't there been some warning sign her parents had missed, some offramp to prevent a lifetime of pain? It left her terrified. Not of *being* divorced — Mom was fine enough, now — but of everything else, everything that came after. All the things she refused to linger on, lest they suck her back down into depression. If you were going to really go all in on someone, shouldn't you be sure?

She glanced at Arnold, his nostrils flaring as Nosferatu lurked in the dark. Could she be sure about Arnold? There *was* something about him. It was indefinable, but there was a goodness to him, a gentleness she didn't see enough of in the world. There was a sadness too, which probably reminded her of Dad in all the worst ways. But she felt safe with Arnold, at home with him in a way she'd never felt before.

You could call that friendship, true — and she'd sure as hell need people to trust if she was going to make it in the city — but you didn't think about people's hands in the dark when they were just friends, did you? You didn't notice the pout to their lips or the dimples around their mouth. You didn't think about their hair or running your hands through it. You—

The credits rolled, the organ playing them out as the lights came up.

"So?" Arnold asked. "Did it live up to your goth teen memories?"

"Hey, I never said I was goth. Sure, I *wanted* to be, but that wasn't gonna fly with my mom. I just had a vampire thing."

She looked down at what remained of the feast they'd put together.

"You were right about the popcorn, though. Even for a baker, I did some serious damage."

"You made it look elegant," he said, laughing.

"Wait," she said, pointing at him as he stood, trying to gather some of their things — most of which could thankfully be recycled, the drinks even served in glass bottles. "Did *you* have a goth phase? You're giving me 'takes one to know one' vibes."

"I'd say I was Midwest emo, but I'm not trying to split hairs."

"Oh my God, you weren't! Did you go to Hot Topic and listen to Taking Back Sunday?"

"Guilty," he said, holding up his hands like he was ready for handcuffs. She wouldn't mind giving him some— *No. No, no, no.*

"What about you?" he asked, joining her by the recycling bin as they carefully sorted their walking disaster. "How did Vampire Helen get her start?"

"We are most certainly not making *Vampire Helen* a thing. But I guess I was an OG — got hooked on *The Little Vampire* first."

"Yessssss!" he cried, holding the door for her. "With that little blond kid from Jerry Maguire? Changed my life."

"Right? So, I started hanging up posters, doing 'research' at the library, all of that. For whatever reason, my gran thought it was hilarious. She could be pretty superstitious with her old-country stuff, but she thought *our* version of vampires was silly. She's not wrong, obviously, but with her enabling me it only got worse. *Interview with the Vampire*, you name it. *Twilight* was basically my own personal apocalypse."

"Made it too cool?"

"*Way* too cool. Don't get me wrong, I was *obsessed* at the time. But once everyone else was hooked… Let's just say it's a long way from pointy-eared Nosferatu to the glittery sexy boys of Forks, Washington."

"Okay, but were you Team Edward or Team Jacob?"

"I'm not answering that," she said, sticking her tongue out at him.

"Alright, then when's your birthday?"

"Why, for my horoscope? I'm an Aquarius rising if you're wondering why I needed to be such an extra-special, unique brand of loser."

He laughed.

"No, no. I was asking so I could give you a vampire cake. Not that my baking will be up to par. But now I *am* curious…"

"All in good time," she said, trying to look dignified and mysterious.

They headed back down Southport, a cool breeze blowing now that night had descended. Still, it somehow felt like summers as a teen, like the night might never end. Something in her *melted* when she talked to Arnold, like the hard shell coming off a candy.

I like him, she thought, her body flushing at the admission.

"Screw it," she whispered to herself.

"What was that?" he asked, looking at her.

She stopped on the sidewalk, grabbing his hand as she pulled him to the side. Her hand felt sweaty all of a sudden, but *his* felt electric, so she hung on to it. He looked down at it, blinking at her in the lamplight.

"I'm sorry if this ruins everything, but can I kiss you?"

"I…" he started, his lips parting. "Yes."

She took his cheek in her hand, her heart pounding, and leaned in, turning her head to the side as her lips met his. They were softer than she'd expected and cooled by the wind. She pressed against him, both of them opening their mouths just slightly. Time disappeared for a moment as they kissed, falling into each other until she thought she might float away.

"This," she said, pulling back just an inch, "is gonna be fun."

———

This was going to be terrible. And amazing, and life-changing, and… Well, it had all come as quite a shock. Arnold was happy, sure, giddy even. But he was also *terrified.*

Arnold sat next to Helen on the train back home, holding her hand. She leaned against him, her head on his shoulder. He closed his eyes, breathing her in. There was a hint of popcorn, but mostly, she smelled like sunshine and flour. It was *heaven*. Still, did he deserve this? Was he even *capable* of deserving this?

He looked around the train car, seeing if there were any spirits. The moment she'd kissed him, the street had burst with color, a flock of spirits raining down on them. Or coming *from* them… It was a type he'd never seen before. They'd been like butterflies, little pink sparks floating in the air. Were they pure emotions? And if so, which one? Were they…love?

He sighed, shaking his head. They'd all but dissipated now. There were a handful of grass spirits, but the train car was mostly quiet. Thankfully, he hadn't seen that giant turtle again. Still, the kiss had created a kind of urgency in him. Nüste's mission had felt different when he was just a new friend helping Helen out. Now, for her sake, he felt like he ought to be at least a *little* surer he hadn't lost his mind. She deserved at least that much, deserved someone who wasn't going to be locked up the moment she—

"Heavy sigh," Helen said from his shoulder. "You alright?"

"Yeah, sorry. It's…a lot to take in."

Just tell her, part of him said. If he was going to do her the disservice of hanging around, or…*dating* her even, then she ought to know as soon as possible how unstable he was. But what if he was *right*? What if the spirits were real? It seemed too good to be true, but he'd already spent so much time swimming in all this make-believe, the larger part of him *did* believe. And if her bakes really were giving him pure feelings, then maybe she'd understand; maybe she'd be the *one* person who didn't push him away for being different.

"No, I'm sorry," she said, letting go of his hand as she swiveled toward him on the seat. "I knew I was rushing things, I knew if I—"

He took her face in his hands and kissed her. He knew he didn't deserve it, but then, why did it feel so right? Why did it feel like being alive for the first time?

"Now we're even," he said as he pulled away.

She blinked. Then, thankfully, she smiled.

"Only if you're sure. I don't wanna scare you off."

"You haven't," he said, squeezing her hand again. No matter what he did next — even if he couldn't find the strength to tell her the truth — he refused to let her think any of this could be her fault. He looked out the window, watching the buildings pass. Night had fallen, and suddenly every home was see-through, a window into another world.

"It's me," he added carefully. He glanced at her, finding her eyes glued to his face. "And I don't mean that in a boring 'it's not you, it's me' kind of way. But like I said the other night, I really wasn't doing well at school. I…cracked, got put in a psych ward."

Despite having talked about it ad nauseam in therapy, he honestly barely remembered that night. It hadn't been a psychotic break, exactly — though he'd met some incredible people in the ward who'd had them and knew the kind of stigma they faced even *using* that word. But from everything his doctors had gathered, he'd just had a *really* terrible panic attack.

Still, it had driven him outside, running in the snow without a coat in the middle of the night. He hadn't been able to explain to the cops what he'd been doing, and before he knew it, he was in handcuffs, being driven to the hospital. Even as he stabilized, he knew he couldn't go back to school, couldn't face the ever-present doubt that he would fail.

"Sorry," he said, realizing he'd stopped talking. But Helen hadn't pulled away. She matched his sad smile, rubbing his arm.

"It's alright, take your time. I can't imagine what you went through. But I don't judge you. I had to be treated for major depression at my first chef job. I…know what that pressure feels like. And, seriously, I *don't* want to put pressure on you now. If this is too much…"

"No, no," he said quickly. How to explain? He didn't want to slam this door shut, didn't want to lose his own silver ring of heaven. After all, if he hadn't wanted to change his life, he would have upped his meds the first time he saw spirits. He wanted his life to change, *needed* it to. It just wouldn't have felt right to kiss her and say nothing.

"I just…wanted you to have the full picture. I know we just met, but I really do like you, and I wanna hang out, and I wanna… I don't know, be a tiny part of your life? I just want to be careful. My mom had to drive all the way to Rhode Island to get me, and she missed so much work, and I just got my life together, and I… Sorry. I don't wanna sound crazy."

"You don't have to use that word," she said. "You're not. *Capitalism* is crazy. Deadlines, finals, and no healthcare is crazy. Let's take it slow. And take care of yourself, alright? Hang out when you want…*kiss* me when you want. Just do what feels healthy."

If only he could be more like Helen. She clearly had her struggles — and he wanted to hear more about them — but she seemed so good at knowing what felt right. He hadn't followed a feeling since he was a child, when his dreams were no further than looking for his Easter basket. Now, he was just a jumbled box of fears and expectations, obsessed with not making any more mistakes. Still, like a magnet pointing north, *something* had drawn him to Helen. Something more powerful than all his doubts.

"*This* feels right," he said, putting his arm around her. "Sorry for being so serious. Let's plan our next hang; I wanna talk about something fun."

"Well, now that you've promised me kayaking, I don't see how we can do anything else. How's Friday?"

"*Promise* is a strong word in Chicago watersports," he said, laughing. "But if it's above sixty, you're on."

She pulled out her phone, giving him an aggressive fist bump when the weather promised to be perfect.

"Sorry," she said, "I'm secretly a total bro."

"Don't be," he said, "I love it. Just remember your backwards hat on Friday."

They finally pulled into the Rockwell stop, and he followed her off to see her to her door. Maybe he also wanted a goodbye kiss — and a long walk home to think about it all. Still, despite the utter terror in his chest, he felt good, hopeful even. And, as they left the train, one last pink butterfly floated off of them, disappearing into the night.

Chapter Twenty-two

Arnold woke up to the same old water stain above his bed, its tendrils unfurling in the sunlight. This time, though, it felt like it might be the most beautiful thing he'd ever seen. In fact, everything seemed to have a shine to it after he and Helen kissed. He wasn't even startled when a herd of mildew spirits appeared on the ceiling, the strange deer creatures walking *upside down* as they wandered through the mold. Unlike the green ones at his uncle's, though, these ones were black with speckles of gray. Did that mean they were a different kind of mold?

"Uh-oh," he said out loud, chuckling.

Maybe his landlord would finally respond to his emails if he mentioned there were spirits growing in the stain. Still, even then — the implications of black mold fresh in his mind — he felt like he could soar. It was like the butterfly spirits of his kiss were inside him, lifting him out of bed with ease. As he sat up, he took his notebook from the bedside table, flipping through the spirits he'd been drawing before bed. He glanced upward, quickly sketching the mold deer.

Something had taken root in him last night, an *optimism* he hadn't felt in years. He tried to hang on to it, that "true north" he'd felt holding Helen's hand on the train. Even seeing spirits didn't feel so absurd anymore. Maybe it was simply warning her about his mental health, but a weight had lifted — or, at the very least, turned into a weight he felt he could carry. It didn't feel like he was slow-walking into doom for once, his future opening up like a door he actually wanted to walk through.

He flipped back through his drawings, marveling at how he'd taken to it after spending so long avoiding art of any kind. He'd become so set on psychology as the only way he could help anyone in his current form, but what if art was still the answer? What about art therapy? Or what about creating without the pressure of going to RISD? He sucked in a slow breath, staring out at the street, the people walking toward the train.

He'd spent the last few years associating his art — his *dream* — with his crisis in Rhode Island. But what if it *wasn't* the art? What if it was just the pressure cooker he'd put himself in? He could still remember when he told Ma he wanted to go to art school. She'd looked…*crestfallen*. After all she'd done to push him — straight A's, valedictorian, scholarship applications — she'd been so disappointed in him.

"That's no career, Arnold," she'd said. "How will you *live*?"

He hadn't had an answer, and yet, he'd still gone through with his RISD application. But at what cost? Ma's words had wormed their way inside him, pushing him to work harder and harder. He *had* to be the best then, had to prove the thing he loved could also be a career. But what did that even mean? Even if he got so good at animating that he got a big job or someone green-lit his work, only the art, the beauty, the *love* could change someone's life the way other artists had changed his. Still, he hadn't been able to see that clearly at the time. And in the end, he'd squeezed his heart so hard it *cracked*, the dream slipping out in the process.

He felt a *weight* on his shoulder and looked down, finding a swirling pink mass there. Slowly, an eye floated in. It was just like Clara's Dream, only a different color — and smaller.

A worthy dream, the spirit said, this voice distinctly male this time. *Thank you.*

Just as quickly, it dissipated, leaving an afterimage in Arnold's eyes. Was that what happened when someone finally dreamt the dream? *Was* he dreaming a dream? Or was he just not afraid to dream his old one anymore? Either way, it all came back to Helen, didn't it? He smiled, flipping open a new page in the notebook. This time, he didn't draw a spirit. He drew *her*, her face coming to him as easily as the sun rose in the sky.

So often, animation was about gestures and abstractions, simplifying the idea of a thing until you could move it across the page. This time, though, it felt like there was no difference between the movement of his pencil and the stunning beauty in his mind. The curves of her face, the dimples, the shining eyes — they all appeared with almost no force applied by his hand. When he was finished, he saw Helen on the page before him.

"Hey," he said, smiling as he leaned down to gently kiss the page. He couldn't believe he'd get to see her again tomorrow. It was like a holy dispensation, a ticket back to heaven every few days. Like a—

His phone buzzed. It was a reminder to leave for school. Underneath it, though, was a string of texts from Ma.

"Take your pills -Love, Ma."

"Arnold?"

"Honey, are you alright?"

Fine, he typed out quickly. *Sorry, just slept in a little.*
Immediately, three dots appeared, showing her typing.
"What about school? Arnold, it'll be midterms any day now!"
I know! Leaving now.
He glanced at the textbook on his desk. He'd *meant* to flip through it the night before, but after kissing Helen, he couldn't bring himself to dive back into the stodgy text. He'd be fine, though, wouldn't he? Even if he had one of those surprise quizzes, it's not like he'd done *none* of the reading, right? Besides, he could muddle through on context clues. Nothing could bring him down!

He shoved everything into his bag, quickly dressing. He swept through the studio, stopping in the kitchen to take his pills. This time, though, he didn't have to eat fortune cookie dust. In the fridge, he had a bag full of day-old croissants from Helen, shoved into his arms as he dropped her off after the movie.

"Good Lord," he said, pulling out one of the perfect, buttery swirls. He shoved it in his mouth, heading for the door. "Dating a baker is making me almost human."

Chapter Twenty-three

By the time Arnold reached the train, he thought he might start skipping. When the train arrived, carrying the giant turtle on its back, he didn't even think of running.

Human child! the turtle cried, its voice like a giant tuba. *I was hoping I might see you again.*

Arnold hadn't honestly gotten a good look at the spirit last time, but it was fascinating. *Turtle* was still the only word that seemed adequate, but it was like the creature's shell had grown up *out of* the metal train. And yet, the skin underneath was still leathery like a reptile's, its head tilting toward Arnold on an ancient neck.

Me too, Arnold thought. *Sorry I couldn't help last time.*

No matter. Though I think you may want to board.

The doors had opened, and everyone else was already filling the train car.

Will we still be able to talk?

Unquestionably, the turtle thought. *The entire train is mine.*

Arnold got on, trying to sit immediately under the turtle's section of the roof. *You can still hear me?* he thought.

Yes, yes, though I'm afraid I must focus between stops.

Why's that? What are you exactly?

The turtle didn't respond for a long time. But as the train pulled in to the

Kedzie stop, it spoke again, the train seeming to vibrate with the sound. How could no one else hear that?

I'm a navigation spirit. We're far prouder than the petty spirits popping up wherever they like. And more useful! Honestly, I don't know how your kind would ever get where they were going without my guidance.

Arnold looked down at the tracks. A train that only ran in one direction didn't *seem* like it needed any help from a navigation spirit, but who was he to question? After all, Poppyseed had appeared due to the *longing* involved in putting a hole in the middle of a bagel.

Was there something you needed from me? Arnold thought, though the train was already leaving for the next station. He settled back, grateful the stops on this section of the Brown Line were only a few blocks apart.

Hmmm, a bit of companionship would suffice, the turtle finally thought. *It's rather rude the way your kind bustles about without so much as a thank you! I'll have you know I used to be worshipped.*

As a subway train? In the sixties?

Bah! Of course not. I've been alive for thousands of years. This shell is just a...recent manifestation. An ornament of my current burdens.

I...see, Arnold thought slowly, nodding. *Well, if you want companions, I do run a cafe. For spirits, I mean.*

Maybe saying he *ran* the cafe was being generous. He still didn't know what had become of Nüste and the grass spirits. Could he afford to take this turtle with him, though? He still had to sit through his classes, and he wasn't planning on seeing Helen until tomorrow. He could always stop by the cafe on his way home, but he'd have to do it without Helen seeing him. He—

There was a sort of *pop* in the air, and he felt a weight appear on his shoulder. He looked down, finding a train circling his shoulders. It was like a tiny toy train, chugging smoke in the air as it wound around on invisible tracks.

I will join you, the turtle said, its voice still coming from above, despite the train on his shoulder.

Well, I guess that's decided, Arnold thought, watching the train climb over one of his backpack straps. At least the thing didn't talk.

———

Nüste ran around the attic, trying to get the cursed grass spirits to let go. Despite their promises to the contrary, they were quickly filling the place, the ten or so blades Arnold had brought quickly turning into hundreds.

Such preference! they all sang in unison every ten minutes or so, apparently convinced the placement of Helen's boxes had some kind of deeper meaning.

It's just junk, you parasites! Let go!

He swatted at them with his essence, something he'd been at for the better part of twelve hours. He kept imagining himself as a pair of giant shears, and each time he battered the grass spirits, he managed to get a dozen of them to dissipate. The problem was, they multiplied so quickly, it hardly seemed to make any difference.

At least each one he exorcised left behind a large amount of spiritual energy. Already, the ceiling was brimming with new supplies, a bright yellow aura floating among Helen's loose emotions up above. Would the girl notice such a sudden abundance of spiritual energy? At least the emotion of seat preference wasn't a dangerous one for her to absorb.

I swear, Arnold, Nüste thought, attracting a blob of rage to peek through the windows. *You're cleaning this up next time you visit.*

———

By the time Arnold got to class, he'd finally learned how to ignore the tiny spirit train — though it *did* occasionally let out a piercing whistle. It had started moving further and further from his shoulders and was currently spiraling down his right leg. He took his usual seat, nodding to the guy next to him. As he started pulling his books out, though, he noticed no one else had anything on their desks.

"Shit," he whispered, his heart skipping a beat.

He looked up at the front of the class, finding "QUIZ!" written in giant chalk letters by the professor. He put his books back, pulling out a pencil. Ironically, the only pencil he'd brought was the same one he'd been using for drawing, the very thing he'd been doing instead of his schoolwork the past few days. Well, that *and* falling for the most incredible woman in Chicago. A bell rang in the hall, signaling the start of the session.

"Alright, everyone," the professor said, smiling as if she weren't about to pass a terrible judgment upon her students. "It's the day you've all been waiting for — quiz three!"

Arnold actually quite liked her — she swore like a sailor and worked at a substance-abuse facility when she wasn't teaching — but at the moment, she looked like doom incarnate. He could do this, though, couldn't he? He'd known the risks, and he'd made choices he found he still agreed with. He could still feel the butterflies inside him from Helen's kiss, could feel the warmth of her hand in his. Besides, who needed perfect grades after high school? It would give him some pastiche to be a low-scoring art therapist. He—

Fuck.

As the quizzes were passed around, he saw the title, "Diagnostic Theory and Neurology." It was on the chapter of the section he hadn't gotten to at all. Not even a little. He'd *glanced* at it just before bed, but when he'd seen a diagram labeling all the parts of the brain, he'd known he'd be hopeless to remember any of it just before falling asleep.

Toot toot! the train whistled, working its way back up the other side of his leg.

I'm glad you agree I'm screwed.

Arnold took a breath, starting to read the questions. If only there were a luck spirit floating about.

Chapter Twenty-four

Helen glanced out the window of the bakery, grateful to find the sun still gloriously blazing in the sky. Only one more day until she saw Arnold, and if the weather held, she'd get her chance at kayaking. It was silly, but she felt the city owed her some time on the water after such a long winter. She'd been a good Chicagoan, bundling up for months, and she was overdue for some sunshine, dammit! Besides, kayaking suddenly had new *romantic* dimensions to offer. Gliding along in a boat with Arnold, his hands on the paddle, kissing him as the turtles waddled by…

Kissing. She sighed, tossing another stick of butter in the mixer. The morning had been spent on "real business," making sure there were enough cookies and coffee to keep the bakery from going under. She'd even had a few more customers than normal. But now, she was trying to get the flavors right on a special bake just for their date — and yes, she *was* calling it a date now. She wanted to bake their first kiss, the flavor having come to her immediately after Arnold left the night before. Unfortunately, it was the hardest flavor she'd come across since all her magic stuff had started.

She closed her eyes, picking up the little bowls of ingredients she'd collected. She sniffed each one in turn, trying to pair them to the flavor in her mind. Like replicating DNA, she had an unzipped prong of genes sitting in her mind, trying to find their matching nucleotides. She took in a deep breath of chocolate, cocking her head. The chocolate wasn't wrong, per se, but it wasn't *right*, either. Who knew kissing could be so complicated? The flavor was light and sweet, but slightly...*musky* too, holding the promise of more desire. There was a playfulness to the flavor, but it wasn't without its bitterness, as if the memory of other heartbreaks was floating in the background.

Her timer beeped, and she turned, stopping the mixer. The base, at least, would be easy. With something this subtle, she didn't dare put the flavor in the batter. She was just going to make some simple rolls, putting the feeling in a glaze over the top. That way, it could be both savory and sweet, allowing for the delicacy of everything she felt crackling on her tongue. Assuming she could figure it out, of course.

She'd pulled out a greenish mango, sniffing at the rind. That seemed more right. She needed something fresh off the tree, a first kiss clearly different than one from a long-term relationship. She set the mango to one side, planning on grating it. Then, she did an eeny-meeny-miney-moe, picking the next ingredient at random. She landed on *garlic* of all things but was surprised when it passed the sniff test. Savory it was, then.

She squatted down, slamming open her salt drawer. She had a pretty wild collection, with salts Gran had left her, joined by ones she'd collected throughout her travels. She grabbed a jar of grayish sea salt flakes from Ireland. For whatever reason, the ocean felt like the right metaphor for their first kiss, like a ship setting sail.

But *were* they setting sail? It was just one kiss! Besides, she'd seen how freaked out Arnold had been on the train, and she didn't want to pressure him. She also had her own fish to fry. Her bakery was just getting off the ground, and she knew she was capable of losing herself in relationships. Arnold *did* seem supportive, but was either of them really in a place to—

Stop! she thought, chiding herself for the hundredth time that day. *Breathe.* She'd had a whole twenty-four hours to think about it, and she'd decided she liked Arnold way too much to give him up so easily. Maybe it *wouldn't* work out, but she wanted to try, all the same. There was no use spiraling for no reason. She hadn't liked anyone like this in a long time, and the rest would simply have to work itself out.

She heard footsteps on the stairs and looked up, finding Em coming into the bakery. Maybe it spoke to how distracted she'd been since that kiss, but she hadn't even realized Em was home. Glancing at Gran's retro cat clock over the door, she realized it was already after three.

"Bit late for you to go to the office, no?"

"Oh my God, I know," Em said, sitting at the table closest to the counter. She looked as posh as ever, somehow managing to be classy in a hot-pink power suit. The outfits alone made Helen think she should have gone into marketing.

"I had a super-early call with the Tokyo office, so my boss said I could come in late."

"But three in the afternoon? Why go at all?"

"Badge swipes," Em said, as if it were obvious. "You have to swipe your keycard a certain number of times per quarter now, but it doesn't matter how long you stay."

Thankfully, Helen had never known corporate life outside of some temp work in school, but it sounded plausible. Even if food service was a meat grinder — alongside every other job in America — at least she didn't have to answer to some soulless McKinsey-addled CEO who only cared about stripping the company of value to raise the dividend.

"This wouldn't have anything to do with the office being closer to that dirtbag's apartment, would it?"

"Don't call him that!" Em said, pulling out her hand mirror to check her makeup, even though she'd just come downstairs. "It *is* convenient, though…"

Em's man-leech lived in the Gold Coast — because, *of course* he did.

"Alright," Helen said, raising her hands in surrender. "I guess I'll just see you Sunday, then." Em spent most weekends at her boyfriend's, so, judging off of the giant bag she'd already packed on a Thursday, she was planning on staying down there a few days. "You here for the roommate tax?"

"Oh, only if you don't mind. We have a reservation tonight — at Girl and the Goat that we made *months* ago — but it's at eight, and if I don't eat now…"

"It's okay," Helen said, laughing. "What do you want?"

She took Em's coffee order, waving her around the counter so she could pick out her own pastry. Unfortunately, she picked a croissant without any emotions in it. She'd been trying to gauge Em's reactions to the magic pastries, though maybe it was wrong to experiment on her roommate.

Em babbled on about her special date night with her boyfriend, apparently happy to ignore the shouting match the two of them had on Tuesday, the yelling barely muffled by the bakery walls. Helen grunted along to the story, trying not to throw her ingredients across the room.

If only he weren't such a tool! Some days it was hard to remember Chicago still had people like that. Buried on the sleepy northwest side as she was, it was all flannels and beer bellies, more Bushwick than Manhattan. Still, Chicago was a world-class city, so presumably *someone* had to be filling up all those music fests and pretentious little Michelin-starred restaurants. But *Em* didn't need that guy! She made her own goddamn money, and she could buy her own fancy dinners and power suits. Wouldn't she be happier with someone nice?

"But what about you?" Em asked, tucking herself back into her chair. "Don't think I haven't noticed *your* situation."

"My…situation?"

"Breathless sighing, hanging around the house like a Victorian lady. Plus, you were gone all Wednesday night. You're *definitely* seeing someone."

"I…" she almost lied, part of her not wanting to jinx things any further. Still, part of her knew she needed to be honest, to voice her crush to the universe before it floated away. She didn't want to force it, to…*manifest* it or something, but Arnold deserved her to speak the words. Like a spell, it would prove she meant everything she'd put inside that kiss.

"Well, I am actually. His name's Arnold, and he's really great. We're going kayaking tomorrow."

"Kayaking? Queen, that is so *you*! I knew you'd find yourself a crunchy man up here."

"Uh…thanks?" Helen said, chuckling as she went back to her bake. She started crisping the garlic on the burner. It was a bit optimistic, assuming she'd find the rest of the ingredients. But at some point in every bake, you had to just go for it.

"That smells good! What is it?" Em asked behind her.

"Making some savory buns for Arnold."

"Oooooh, so you like *love* him. You never baked for that Tinder guy."

"Tinder guy was a monster," Helen said, moving the garlic around with a spatula. "But…he *is* special, I think. I just don't want to screw it up. After everything we've both been through—"

"Can I give you some advice?" Em interjected, coming around the counter to put her dishes in the sink. It was still too much of a stretch to get her to wash them after roommate tax, but she probably didn't want to get soap on her hot-girl outfit, either. Em leaned against the fridge, watching Helen cook.

"You're obviously such a boss — and like, thank you for letting me live here — but you were brave enough to do your bakery, so why not this? At some point you have to…I dunno, turn the oven on, right? You might burn the place down, but it's not like you can bake in the freezer."

Helen raised an eyebrow. Em just shrugged.

"That's…really good advice, actually."

"Right? *Man-leech* thinks I don't know anything, but I'm really good at my job. Besides, you have to have hope, you know? You—"

Helen usually had a rage blackout at the sound of Em's boyfriend's name — his name automatically replaced in her mind by its true form. But hearing what the bastard had *said*, that Em didn't "know anything," she almost had another. She marched up to Em, pointing the rubber spatula in her face — barely managing not to splatter garlic on the power suit.

"Break. Up. With. Him."

"Oh my God, you're so dramatic," Em said, laughing, though it sounded forced. "He's not *that* bad…"

"He *is* that bad. Tell me what table you're at tonight, and I'll come bludgeon him with a rolling pin."

"I think you actually might," Em said, eyes wide. "At least I know you have my back, roomie."

She gave Helen a shoulder hug, waving as she grabbed her bag and skipped toward the door. Helen pinched her brow, trying to get her blood pressure to return to normal. Still, even with her rage, Em's advice floated through her mind. *You have to have hope.*

Nutmeg, she thought.

She slammed around the cupboard, pulling out some nutmeg to add to the garlic. When that was done, she could add the mango peel and a hint of sugar and… *And the recipe was done.* She only had to hope a kiss-flavored bun would keep whatever this magical, terrifying thing was she had with Arnold was going. She—

She just caught the flash of someone passing by the bakery. Some who looked remarkably like Arnold.

Helen dashed for the door, her heart soaring at the thought of seeing him a day early. How nice it would be for him to surprise her! If only her buns were ready!

When she got outside, though, there was no one there. She looked back and forth, finding the street empty.

"Man, I really got it bad."

She chuckled, heading back into the bakery. Whatever happened next with Arnold, it couldn't be a bad sign if she was imagining him everywhere.

Chapter Twenty-five

When Arnold got back to his apartment building, his heart was still pounding. He'd stopped by the bakery to drop off the turtle train, and Helen had almost seen him. He'd caught just a glimpse of her rushing to the door before he ducked into the alley, slamming against the brick wall. It was a foolish thing to do — what if she'd seen him hiding there? — but his instincts had taken over. He couldn't just pop by, not when things were so new between them! Still, hiding in an alley behind the bakery was infinitely creepier, wasn't it?

He'd stood stock-still in the alley, waiting for Helen to go back into the bakery as Nüste yelled at him from above. Actually, Nüste hadn't *stopped* yelling since the moment Arnold got off the train, the little mushroom's voice joined by a chorus of grass spirits laughing in the attic.

You've really done it this time, kid! Nüste had shouted down at him. *I can't make them stop!*

Still, despite the chaos in the attic, the turtle's train had managed to leave Arnold's shoulder. For the first time all day, the turtle's voice had returned, replacing the random whistling of the train.

What fun this is! the turtle's voice cried from the attic. *Thank you, child.*

It's not fun! Nüste had yelled. *If we don't get them out of here, you can't have any tea.*

Oh dear, the turtle had said, somehow tempted by whatever strange tea Nüste

106

was brewing. The turtle joined Nüste in his shouting, his voice echoing through the neighborhood. *Out, vile spirits! Out, damn you!*

The grass spirits finally let go, dozens of them flying out through the roof, laughing as they dissipated.

Finally back home, Arnold stopped at his mailbox, chuckling to himself. Creepiness aside, all this spirit stuff *was* actually getting kind of fun. Still, hopefully he could free Nüste — and Helen — soon. He couldn't keep sneaking around like this, not when he already had a dozen other things to juggle. He shook his head, starting up the stairs. He'd *bombed* that quiz, the logic of the multiple-choice questions eluding him until the very end. But it was just one quiz, wasn't it? He could probably make it up without failing the course. He just had to knuckle down. He—

"There you are!" Lois said, coming down the stairs just as he was going up them. "Come with me."

"But I..." he started, looking in the direction of his apartment. He'd had every intention of starting on the next section of his textbook right away. Between work and seeing Helen tomorrow — on an actual date and *not* lurking in her alley — he really had no choice but to do schoolwork every moment he wasn't sleeping.

"No arguments," Lois said, beckoning over her shoulder as she walked past him. "It's worth it, I promise."

By the time he got back through the front door, Lois was already halfway down the block. She walked with a cane, but she seemed like she had no need for it, moving quickly in the direction of the square.

"Can I ask where we're going now?" Arnold said, finally catching up with her.

Lois smiled, a gold tooth glinting in her mouth. It reminded him of his own grandmother.

"Gene's — at least at first. We have to pick something up."

Already, he could see Gene's on the horizon. A fifty-year-old Polish deli, it had a giant statue of a cow on the awning. In the summer, they had a biergarten on the roof, and he vaguely remembered going up there for hot dogs with his dad as a kid. Lois took him inside, marching up to the deli counter, where rows and rows of sausages hung from the ceiling. There was no one else there in the middle of the day, so Lois didn't take a number, flagging down the nearest man in a white deli hat.

"What can I get you?"

"A dozen *ćevapi*, cooked."

The man nodded, heading for a tray of what looked like meat logs.

"Cha...boppy?" Arnold asked, trying to repeat what she'd said.

Lois nodded, pointing at the sign. It read *Ćevapi* in big letters.

"My husband was a Croat, remember? These were his favorite."

"Case-less sausage," the deli man said, handing them over in wax paper. "It's like a *kafta*; you're gonna love it."

After they paid and went back to the street, Lois turned *away* from their apartment building.

"What now?" Arnold asked, following her.

"You're gonna help me ride the bus. I hate doing it alone."

They waited for the 49, Lois leaning against the brick wall of the pet food store.

"So, how are you?" Lois asked, looking him over.

"That's it? No big reveal, just 'how are you?'"

"Sure," she said, laughing. "Don't leave an old woman waiting."

Arnold smiled.

"Good, I think," he finally said, cocking his head. "Maybe even *really* good, though I did fail a quiz today — quite spectacularly, actually."

"Ah," Lois said, smiling. "You're in love, then?"

"It's that obvious? What if I'm just lazy?"

"Would lazy carry a hundred pounds of soil to the roof for an old lady?"

"Fair," he said, laughing. "There *is* a girl, but that's not the only reason I failed. I started drawing again — I used to study art — and I've been…a bit distracted lately. I'm a little nervous, honestly. If I flunk out…"

"My husband was an artist," Lois said. "Anything I can see?"

Normally he was shy about his art — especially with someone whose husband had been a *real* artist — but something about Lois made him feel like he could share. He pulled out his notebook, handing it to her. Perhaps failing the quiz shouldn't have been such a surprise. As she flipped through the pages, he realized just how many pages he'd filled in the past few days.

"These are lovely," Lois said, absorbed by the notebook until she reached the last page where he'd drawn Helen. "Ahhh, and so is she. What's her name?"

"Helen," he said, feeling like he was reciting a spell.

"Beautiful name. Seems like a nice girl."

"You can tell from a drawing?"

"Oh, yeah. I can tell lots of things. Decided I would marry my husband just by seeing him through a window."

The bus came, one of the light-blue electric ones the city was piloting.

"Come on," Lois said, returning the notebook. "Help me climb these stairs."

It wasn't until they transferred to the Devon bus that Arnold realized where they were going. While nowhere near as massive as the Rosehill Cemetery where he'd met the moss spirit, St. Henry's still took up almost an entire city block. The steeple of the church rose above the buildings of Little India, the red brick glowing in the afternoon sun.

"We're going to see your husband?" he asked.

She smiled, nodding as she yanked on the bus's pull cord. Arnold helped her up, holding the ćevapi. As soon as they were off the bus, Lois took off into the grass, back to walking at her usual speed. She wove between the gravestones, looking like Ms. Pac-Man as she navigated the most efficient route. Finally, they ended up at a simple marble headstone, the kind with an extra space for Lois's name someday. On top of it, there was another mossy spirit, this one with a dull pink color. In fact, it looked exactly like the one that had appeared on his shoulder that morning. Was it because Lois's husband had been an artist too?

I know you, the spirit said, one of its eyeballs floating into view.

You were her husband's dream? Arnold asked, stooping down to help Lois as she pulled weeds from around the grave.

And the dream of many others. I haven't been here long.

Arnold looked at the headstone, finding the date only a few years in the past.

"Your husband's name was Emil?" Arnold asked Lois, reading the name.

"Yep. Emil and Lois. Not bad, eh?"

Arnold nodded, returning to the spirit.

What was Emil's dream?

It was common, in a sense, the spirit thought. *You can see I'm nearly gone, drifted to new hearts. But this man felt his strongly, I think.*

It was true. Whereas Clara's Dream had covered the entire headstone, Emil's Dream only grew on a few square inches of the marble surface.

And what dream was that? Arnold thought.

Why, love, of course.

"Hand me the ćevapi," Lois said, groaning as she used the headstone to stand back up.

"Do we…leave it here?" Arnold asked.

"You know how many rats live in this city?" she asked, laughing. "We eat it."

She took a tissue from her purse, scooping up a handful of the ćevapi and handing it to him. She took some for herself, setting the rest of the package down.

"To you, baby," she said to the gravestone, cheers'ing her sausage against the marble.

"To Emil," Arnold echoed, eating one. It was rich and juicy, rather like a sausage-shaped meatball.

They stood that way for a while, eating ćevapi, a soft breeze blowing through the cemetery.

"You know, Arnold," Lois finally said, patting his shoulder. "I think you're going to be just fine. Don't worry about school."

"What makes you say that?"

"I've lived a long time, and I've lost my best friend. Whatever you're doing with this Helen girl, I'm sure it's a good use of time."

"Even if it means she winds up with a dropout?"

"Especially then. Heck, Emil was *engaged* when I saw him through that window. We were together fifty-five years. Caused quite the uproar in the beginning, but people adjust."

"He was lucky to have you," Arnold said.

Lois smiled, taking the last ćevapi. She dug a little hole in the grass next to the grave, slipping the sausage in. She raised a finger to her lips, signaling Arnold should keep her secret.

"You bet your ass he was."

Chapter Twenty-six

The next day, Arnold came out of his apartment feeling like a new man. He'd be going straight to Helen's from the record store, and he'd spent way longer than he'd like to admit picking out his clothes. Choosing between the same pair of jeans and two different button-downs shouldn't have taken an hour, but tonight felt special. It was a date, and he *knew* it was a date.

He was locking the door behind him when his phone buzzed. He saw Ma's name and assumed it would be her usual message telling him to take his pills. But as he opened it, he found only two words.

Come over.

I have work, he typed. *Can I come after?*

He stood there in the hallway, frowning as Ma typed.

Now.

He hurried for the stairs, his mind racing as he wracked his brain for what it could be about. He should have been more worried about something being wrong with Dad or something, but all he could do was assume he was in trouble for something. But what? He felt the weight of his backpack on his shoulders, the notebook inside. Could she somehow know about the drawings? Had someone from the animation club posted a picture with him in it?

He hopped on a Divvy bike, crossing the blocks between his house and theirs at breakneck speed. Even as he opened the back door with his key, though, he still had no clue. She was waiting for him in the kitchen, the coffee machine gurgling behind her. Ma had her glasses on the edge of her nose, making her look like some combination between a mole and a shark, both deadly and ridiculous.

"Sorry," he said, "I didn't—"

"Sit."

He sat instantly, barely even pulling out the chair as he dropped into it with a thud. There were grass spirits in it, but he ignored their laughter. Ma had her tablet out in front of her, and she turned it, sliding it toward him. The moment he saw his school's logo, his stomach dropped. He'd forgotten she had access to his grades. He didn't even need to look at the screen to know what was on it. Still, the grade from his quiz, and its red text, shined like blood.

"Listen," he started, even knowing it was a mistake.

"Listen?" she asked, her hands balling into fists. "Arnold all we *do* is listen. You want to go to art school, we let you. You need me to come get you, I came. You want to live alone, I don't stop you. But you were supposed to tell me if you weren't fine. You were supposed to take your pills. This doesn't *look* like fine."

It crashed over him like a wave, each word a stone dragging him back into the sea he'd finally crawled out of.

"But I *am* fine. I'm great, actually. It was just a mistake. I mixed up the day of the quiz, and—"

"*Mixed up*? Arnold, you think your dad can mix up his shift at work and get away with it? Tiny slips become big slips. Don't you remember? My baby boy ran out in the cold with no shirt on all because he picked something silly over a steady life. You don't just *mix up* your second chance, Arnold. What could you possibly be doing now that's more important than school?"

Arnold said nothing, the answers more damning for their truth. Dating, drawing, *seeing spirits*. None of them were good answers. None of them even sounded right as the memories crashed back down around him.

"Can you tell me honestly that you're alright? That you're not losing touch again?"

Could he? He'd leapt at the chance to change his life, to chase Nüste down the rabbit hole. He *believed* in it, all of it. But what evidence did he have that he was right?

"No," he said. "I mean… I don't know."

"You don't *know*? What am I supposed to do, Arn? Am I supposed to call Miss Lisa?"

"No," he said quickly, his pulse jumping again, awakened from the stupor of his dressing down. Miss Lisa was the name of the administrator at the inpatient clinic they'd put him in when he got back to Chicago. She was a doctor, a clinical psychologist, but Ma had latched onto the nickname, Miss Lisa, that she used with her patients. Ma couldn't check him in against his will, though, could she? Not when he was an adult, not after the medical hold on him from Rhode Island had expired.

Still, part of him was afraid he'd agree to go on his own, to lock himself away instead of facing what a failure he'd become. After all, wasn't she right? *Wasn't* he losing touch? But if he was, why was Helen still shining in his mind like the sun at the center of the universe? He thought of Lois, of how happy she'd seemed just looking at Emil's grave. Wasn't Helen worth all this? Or was he putting her at risk too? It wasn't like he could date her from a psych ward.

"Then what do you propose we do, Arnold? Do you think life will go easy on you because of your problems?"

It was one of Ma's favorite lines, one she'd learned from *her* father. Arnold could hardly remember the man, but his sacrifices were legend in the family, everything he'd given up to get their family to Chicago. He'd worked two jobs, three jobs, a million jobs, gone on nights and weekends, anything to keep his family fed. He'd been the one who pushed Ma to become an optometrist's assistant. And what of Ma's sacrifices? She'd done everything for him, given him every opportunity, and he'd spit on it. Helen and spirits aside, he wasn't even taking school seriously.

Even knowing how close he'd come to losing everything, knowing how lucky he was to have a family to bail him out, he hadn't worked anywhere near as hard as he should have. He *loved* animation, but was Ma even wrong about how silly his dreams were? The world could be a dark place, and even if he wished he could change that, he knew just how close he'd come to the edge. Where would he be if his grandfather hadn't sacrificed so much, if his parents hadn't bailed him out?

Arnold felt his old self sliding back into place. Like a door slamming shut, the light from Helen's sun felt distant, cut off. Ma sank back into her chair, shaking her head. She squeezed her forehead, looking like she'd nearly popped a blood vessel.

"Don't you *want* to do well?" she asked. This time, her tone was softer, her eyes losing their fire until only a sort of sadness remained. That was even harder to take. It reminded him of when they'd released him from the hospital, her eyes as she glanced at him on the long drive home from Rhode Island, no longer recognizing her own son.

"I do. I'm sorry. I just got distracted, I swear. It won't happen again."

He felt a weight shift inside him, a flash of light appearing just outside his vision. He looked over at his shoulder, where a black ball had appeared. It seemed to swirl, its surface covered in ridges like a musket ball, like something forged inside a fire.

"I have to go to work," he finally said, his throat dry. "I'll talk to my professor. It's gonna be fine, I promise."

"Okay," she said, dismissing him with a wave of the hand. "I made a lunch for you in the fridge."

She'd probably made it for herself before she sat down to use her tablet, but the gesture still cut him to his core. She loved him — as much as she knew how, anyway, as much as anyone could love such a sorry excuse for a son.

"Thanks, Ma," he said, forcing himself to stand, pulling the paper bag from the fridge. "Love you."

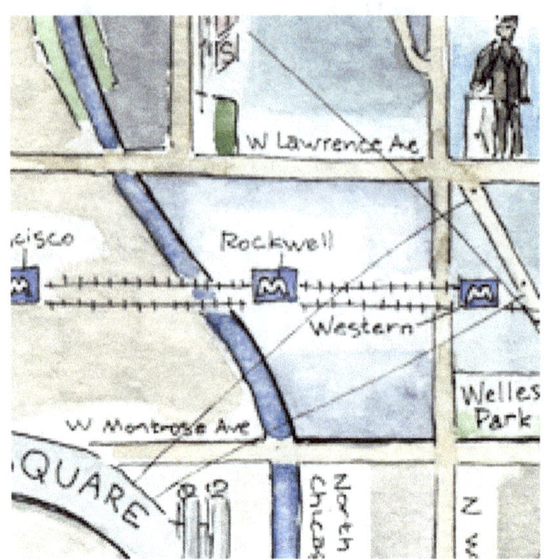

Chapter Twenty-seven

Before Helen knew it, it was closing time. She'd had a surprising number of customers — or at least a surprising number for her. One of them had even asked for one of the kiss buns she'd made for Arnold, having noticed them on the counter while she was browsing the bakery case.

"What is that? It looks amazing!"

"It's a…kiss," she said, unable to lie quickly enough. "Er…a *petit bise*. They're all the rage in…France?"

"Well, I'll absolutely have one of those!"

Helen put her best customer smile on her face, moving to bag up one of the buns. It felt wrong to give away one of Arnold's kisses. Still, it wasn't like he needed a *dozen* kiss buns — even if she was planning on giving him more than a dozen real-life kisses.

The customer walked straight out the door with the bun, so she'd have to wait and see if the magic worked. Of course, if she made all of Chicago start kissing each other, she could have a lawsuit on her hands. Ideally, they'd wait until they had someone appropriate to kiss, though she couldn't rule out people spontaneously kissing like it was V-day. She was very far from having lawsuit money, but between the dozen or so customers she'd had, she'd at least made enough to cover her expenses for once.

She went to flip the sign to *closed*, eager to shower before her date, when her phone dinged. She pulled it from her apron to find a calendar reminder, a horrible, untimely curse of a calendar reminder. *Therapy*, it said. She had an hour and a half until Arnold arrived, which meant, after therapy, she'd only have a half hour to shower and look presentable.

She must have been the only person in Chicago who scheduled therapy on a Friday afternoon — a testament to how depressing her social life had been before Arnold — but she couldn't cancel now. She'd already made her therapist wait around on a Friday, and that was before considering the cancellation fee.

Helen stopped in the middle of the cafe, taking what she hoped was a deep, calming breath. She could do this. She'd just skip washing her hair. Arnold could take a bit of bakery hair, couldn't he?

"He'd fucking better," she muttered to herself, fumbling behind the counter for her computer. She was basically a goddess of baking, and if he didn't like the smell of cookies, he simply wasn't the man for her. She pulled out the stool she kept by the cash register and flipped her screen open, clicking the button for the patient portal before she could regret it.

"Dr. Laura, hi!" she said, basically screaming, a giant fake smile on her face.

"Helen, nice to see you," the doctor said.

She was a fashionable middle-aged lady, with giant, chunky glasses and a different necklace at every appointment. She must have had hundreds of them, today's a dazzling mix of black beads and dancing golden cats. Helen always wanted to ask about them, but she didn't want to pry. After all, part of what they were working on was her people-pleasing, an instinct that threatened to manifest into asking her therapist a million questions, even though she'd paid for the session.

"I see we're taking the appointment from the bakery again?"

"Oh, uh…yeah," Helen said, looking around her as if she hadn't noticed. "Sorry."

"No need to apologize," Dr. Laura said with an enigmatic half-smile. "The time is yours to use as you choose. I just wanted to note it. You mentioned last time you felt like you never had time for yourself?"

Dr. Laura was right, of course. And in that, she was the perfect therapist for Helen. She was tough, maybe even a little cold, but in a weird way, it kept Helen from trying too hard. She'd always wanted her other therapists to like her, which quite easily got in the way of her progress. But Dr. Laura was impossible to please. Not difficult or mean, just…*blank*. There was a kind of freedom in that.

"Right," Helen said, nodding. "But I swear this time is different. I have a *date*."

She said the word as if she'd written in glitter pen, as if she could summon a boyfriend like a schoolyard game of M.A.S.H.

"Well, that's interesting," Dr. Laura said, nodding as she took some notes. What did those notes say about her? Was she just writing "delusional" over and over again as she pretended to listen?

"And I'll want to hear all about that, but first, let's pick up where we left off last time. How are you doing with the self-compassion exercises?"

Right, self-compassion. *Not* her strong suit. She did yoga. She occasionally meditated. It wasn't lost on her that self-compassion — like everything else in life — was a practice. But something about staring at herself in the mirror and saying nice things felt too self-indulgent for her to do regularly.

"I'm…trying," she said. "But isn't it kind of silly? I mean, women are being punched in the face on the street, and I'm supposed to whisper sweet nothings to myself in the bathroom? I don't feel like I've done anything to deserve it."

"Do you think those women deserve to be punched in the face?"

"Obviously not!" Helen said, wanting to throw her computer. "But shouldn't I be helping? Doing something for someone else?"

"Maybe. But answer me this — *why* don't they deserve to be punched in the face?"

"Because they're human beings! Because we have rights. Because the patriarchy is a lie. Because… Because they shouldn't need a reason!"

"Then why do *you* need a reason?"

Helen threw up her hands. But for what? Dr. Laura was right. She slowly lowered them, letting out a sigh.

"Point taken."

"Thank you," Dr. Laura said. "But this isn't debate club. I want you to really think about this. Compassion isn't zero sum. All suffering is bad and equally worthy of attention. You have to start with a mindset of abundance. Caring for yourself isn't taking resources away from someone more needy. It's making you strong enough to do the great work you're already doing for the world."

"*Am* I doing great work, though? I know the little voice inside my head is toxic, but it pushes me. My mom always said if I'm not criticizing myself, then someone else will do it for me. I have to…I don't know, *try* at least."

Dr. Laura nodded at that, taking some notes, which made Helen want to scream. But it also made her double back, thinking through again exactly what she'd said.

"Why does dough rise?" Dr. Laura finally asked.

"Uh…yeast? Sugar? Heat?"

"So, certain conditions are necessary?"

"Sure. I mean I get what you're trying to say. But you also have to knead the bread, don't you? Seems like a mixed metaphor."

"Fair," Dr. Laura said with a chuckle. "Maybe I shouldn't have used baking — that's your territory. Let me try something else. You like to read, don't you?"

She nodded.

"What makes you read those books? Is there a test at the end?"

"No. I just like it."

"And what about this date you're going on? Do you think this person will make you more successful? Will they force you to help more people?"

"No," she said, resigned — and avoiding the impulse to roll her eyes.

"You're a good person, Helen. You can trust your intrinsic motivation. If you take the pressure off, maybe you'll see you actually have the energy to do all these things that are so important to you."

"Okay," she said, nodding. "Can I tell you about my date now?"

"Please," Dr. Laura said, opening her palms as if inviting Helen's descent into frivolity.

"Well, his name is Arnold. And let me tell you, I like him so much, I actually wish I were showering right now."

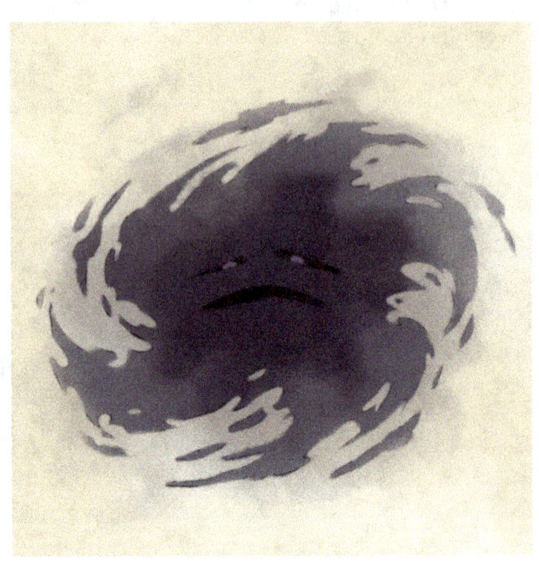

Chapter Twenty-eight

Arnold spent his shift at work trying to detox from seeing spirits — at least until he could find a way to up his meds. He'd let this whole thing go on long enough, and he couldn't let it go any further. It had all felt so real — so much realer than anything he'd ever experienced — but the entire dream had run into a concrete wall when confronted by Ma. It was a reminder of the truths he'd been avoiding. Namely, that he'd gone down the rabbit hole before, and without his parents to pull him out, he might never have escaped.

On his walk to the store, he'd seen some strange vine-like spirits growing from trees, but he avoided looking at them directly. Now, he was pointedly avoiding going in the back, where the dust spirit lived. Even if Jimmy showed up, he'd refuse to go look for more Grateful Dead records. All he had to do was mind his business and make it through his shift.

There was a weight to him now, a *heaviness* he hadn't felt in months. He shoveled Ma's lunch into his mouth, barely tasting it. He just didn't want any more of her hard work to go to waste. Meanwhile, the thing on his shoulder only grew. He'd thought it would grow eyes or legs, but oddly, it didn't. It remained the same, a whirling black orb like a black hole in miniature. It even tugged at his shirt with its unseen vacuum.

Was it not a shame spirit, then? Maybe it was— *No.* He refused to let himself get curious about it. Even thinking about spirits brought Ma's voice rushing back into his mind, asking him why he'd throw away the life she'd worked so hard to give him. He could almost picture her marching down the street, an army of doctors at her back.

"Why did you do this to me?" she asked, her eyes full of tears.

"Yes, yes," the doctors murmured behind her, looking over their clipboards. Even worse was the voice he imagined last, emerging from the back of the crowd — Helen.

"You *lied* to me," she whispered, heartbroken.

He shook his head, trying to focus on the catalogue in front of him. Daydreams wouldn't solve his problems. If he wanted to make this right, he'd simply have to get better. He had to stop indulging in fantasies, stop seeing things that weren't there. He had to give the people in his life the version of him they deserved. Even if — in the case of one particularly notable, beautiful woman — the best version of him might be none at all.

He sighed, putting a price tag on one of the new movies he'd ordered for the store, *Princess Mononoke*. It was one they'd had before, obviously — one of the first he'd stocked — but they'd *actually* sold out, one of the first times he'd felt like Tony had understood what Arnold was trying to do with his "little cartoons."

Arnold held the box in his hand, tracing the images on the back with his finger. It showed Ashitaka riding his elk. Cursed by a demon, he'd been forced to leave his home in search of the gods. Arnold never thought he'd relate so strongly to a hero like that. He'd always lacked the skills and courage of a hero, but today, he *did* at least feel cursed. Whatever this illness was, crowding his mind with things that weren't there, he felt forever marked by it, forced to go on a journey he didn't want to take. But maybe, for Helen, he could be courageous just this once. Maybe he could find the strength to set her free.

———

By the time he reached Helen's, Arnold wasn't sure if he could take another step. He'd avoided the train for obvious "spirits-aren't-real" reasons, but that had only served to give him more time to rehearse what he was going to say — a rehearsal that never ended without tears coming to his eyes. He didn't *want* to do this, but it was the only way, the only chance he had left of doing the right thing. This was all his fault, and even if it left him in tears, it was a small price to pay for keeping Helen safe, free of his instability.

Unfortunately, the orb on his shoulder was only growing larger, making it hard to focus on anything else — even as he stared down at the sidewalk to avoid seeing any other random spirits. Was it possible it was this thing weighing him down? His legs felt like lead, like he'd been dragging a stone down Leland Avenue, knocking into the gardens where people grew all their lovely little pollinator plants. He shut his eyes, pressing onward. Maybe once he said his piece, this spirit would disappear.

Hey! a voice shouted in his mind.

Arnold gritted his teeth. He wasn't sure if he'd see Nüste or not, but now he wished he could have avoided the spirit entirely, the clearest example of his mind making things up. It was this spirit that had kicked everything off, that had made him start sneaking around.

Hey! I'm talking to you, buster. You seriously gonna walk on by after all we've been through?

Arnold looked up, catching a glimpse of the spirit in the attic. He looked unchanged, the little mushroom cap bobbing in the window. He didn't see or hear the turtle.

"I'm sorry," he said out loud. He'd gotten so much better at speaking in his mind, but now he couldn't seem to manage it. "I just came to say goodbye. I can't do this anymore."

Oh, Arnold, Nüste said, sighing. *What have you done? Your third eye is barely open. And— Wait...what is that?*

Arnold looked at the spirit on his shoulder. The spiraling black orb had nearly tripled in size since the morning, growing until it was nearly halfway up his neck.

Arnold, that's a—

"I don't want to know," Arnold said, raising a hand — and earning a look from a dog walker. He clenched his teeth. "I'm sorry, but I can't keep pretending this is real. I can't afford it. Whether you're real or not, I'm… I'm sorry."

He started walking toward the bakery again, unsure if he could even make it the next hundred yards.

Arnold, look, I can see you're not well. Why don't you take a break? Rest up? I've been working you hard, I know, but what's a few weeks off compared to an eternity? Just turn around right now. Please. That spirit is no good. I can't have you leaving that here. Helen can't take it.

Arnold froze, his hand on the door. What *was* the spirit on his shoulder? Would it really hurt Helen if he brought it here? The one impulse he'd had all along — aside from trying to free himself from his boring, miserable life — had been to help her. And yet, he'd been sneaking around her building, hiding in her alley. *He* was the real danger, not some made-up spirit. Leaving was the only thing he could do to help her now. This wasn't real. It *wasn't* real.

"I'm sorry, Nüste," he said, fighting back the tears. "I'm done."

He walked into the store, ready to do what he should have done from the beginning.

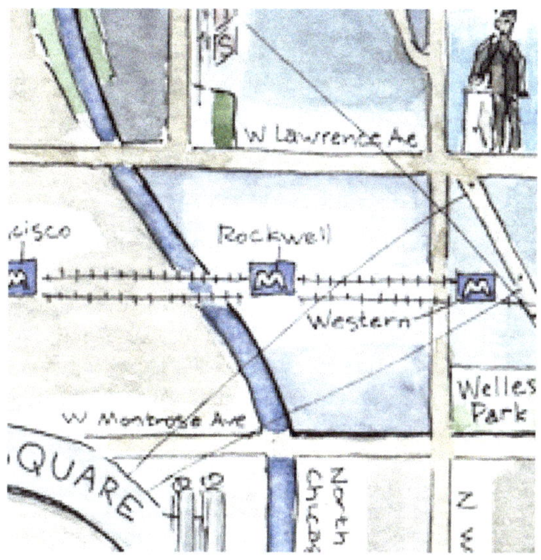

Chapter Twenty-nine

By the time she saw Arnold, Helen felt ridiculous. She fluffed up her hair and straightened her shirt, picking up the tray of buns. What was this, *I Love Lucy*? This was radical baking, dammit! She wouldn't just lock herself in the kitchen, baking for some man! Of course, she actually *wanted* to bake for this man. Still, she didn't move, holding the pose despite its absurdity. She would deliver her beautiful little kiss buns, and she wouldn't feel bad about it.

As Arnold crossed the street, though, he didn't look like someone who needed a cookie — he looked like he needed a hug. His head was bowed, his eyes heavy. It looked like his backpack held only boulders, as if each step cost him something dear. Was something wrong? Or was this how he always looked out in the world? She'd never seen him approach before, her head always stuck in the oven or the fridge. He'd always just appeared like some beautiful little angel.

She rolled her shoulders, resuming her "sexy" bakery pose. She hated herself just a tiny bit for glancing at her cleavage, but what was the point of wearing a date-night shirt if you couldn't enjoy looking a little hot? It was probably too soon to hope for anything spicy to happen with Arnold, but a girl could dream, couldn't she? Besides, if these cookies really did contain the magic of a kiss, he'd probably swoon into her arms the moment he—

Arnold stopped by the door, looking up. She raised an eyebrow, setting down the buns as she came around the counter. Was there something wrong with her roof? As Arnold came into view again through the window, though, she noticed his mouth was moving. He shook his head, squeezing his eyes shut. Was there…someone in the attic? Her eyes swiveled over to the ceiling, trying to see through the floorboards. It made her shudder, thinking of the attic, the shadow of all the things she'd hid there looking down at her.

But then, thankfully, the wicked spell was broken, the bell over the door banishing it with its chime as Arnold came in.

"What were you doing out there?" she asked, smiling. "Saying your prayers you'll get lucky tonight?"

"Oh," he said, glancing above him, his own smile half-hearted and nervous. "Sorry. I… Well, I guess that's what I wanted to talk to you about."

She felt her stomach drop, sparing a glance for her poor buns. Part of her wanted to reach for them like a life raft, to salvage the feeling they'd had the other night. But she could also tell it was too late, their *Titanic* sinking and leaving only a little door to cling to. But was she Rose in this situation or Jack?

"Uh, come in," she said quietly, gesturing toward one of the tables. Just moments ago, she'd wanted to grab him, to cover him with kisses and stuff him full of baked goods. Now, he just looked small, shrinking in on himself as he took a chair, his fists in tight balls. She moved to join him in the other chair when he started talking.

"I don't think I can see you anymore. I'm sorry."

There it was. At least the blow was instant. From what she knew of him, though, it meant he'd been thinking about it long and hard. How long had he known? Wednesday? The movie theater? Had she destroyed this fledgling thing between them so easily, crushing it before it took flight? She sat across from him, calmer than she should be. After all, what was the point in making a scene? This was her fault, wasn't it?

"No, *I'm* sorry," she found herself saying. "I shouldn't have kissed you."

In part, it was true. She shouldn't have pressed him. People were an ocean, a galaxy, a cave of riches, and she only knew an inch of Arnold. And, even seeing the pain behind his eyes, she'd pushed ahead anyway. On the other hand, that *was* only in part. The other half of her wanted to shake him, if only to force him to see that this — whatever it was — was *good*. Couldn't he feel it? Didn't he sense it?

"It's not that," he said squeezing his forehead. "Please, don't think that. I'm…messed up. I wasn't going to tell you this, but I can't let you think that you…"

He shook his head, sucking in a breath.

"I'm seeing things, Helen. Tiny spirits. I thought they were real, but now, I don't know. I failed a test, and—"

"Arnold, you failed a test? Oh my God, I'm so sorry. You could have studied here. I could have helped you. I…"

She trailed off. Of *course*, she apologized for his test, proving the people-pleaser in her, even as she ignored the rest. But what about that other part? It seemed to catch up to her all at once. He was *seeing* things? She didn't judge him for it — there was nothing scary about Arnold — though it made her feel even guiltier. Leave it to her to meddle in someone's crisis, throwing herself at them at their lowest point. And was she really any better? She actually believed she could bake her feelings. Wasn't that just as frightening?

"No, no, that's the point," he said, looking like he might cry. "It's… Helen, I can't be with *anyone*. I like you, so, *so* much, but I'm scared. And my parents… I can't do this to them. But it's *not* your fault. The past few weeks have been amazing, I just… I have to get better, I'm sorry."

He stood, turning toward the door.

"Wait," she said, leaping from her chair. "Can't I help you? You said you're seeing things? Spirits? Did you see one here?"

Part of her was afraid. What if her attic really was haunted? If it was a ghost, it would probably be the only person in her family with unfinished business, the one who'd *blame* her for what she'd done. Still, she wasn't asking only for herself. She wanted to understand, *needed* to. She would let him go, wouldn't hold him to a kiss, but couldn't she be his friend? Couldn't she do *something* for him?

Arnold glanced up at the ceiling again, setting his jaw. "No. I…uh…I haven't seen anything here. It's not important, not when I know it's not real."

He took off his backpack, pulling out a notebook. He held it in his hands, looking at it. Finally, he put it down on the table in front of her.

"I hope this helps you understand. I…think I just have to fix my meds, figure all this out. But I'll go now, okay? I'm so sorry."

"Just give me a hug first. I'll be your friend if you want."

She opened her arms, and he looked at her, glancing at one hand then the other, no doubt wondering if he wanted to be smothered by the person who'd stressed him out so badly in the first place. But a second later, he approached, melting into her as he hugged her back. She squeezed him tighter than she should have, trying to give him something of her strength even as she took his for herself. It only lasted a moment before he pulled away.

"Goodbye, Helen."

The doorbell chimed again, ringing against a silence that suddenly felt too deep, like the bakery had been flung out into space, the city falling away. And as Arnold left, he seemed to pull the air out of her heart behind him. She sank back into her chair, barely reaching it as the first sob hit her. She buried her face in her hands, unable to hold the tears back any longer.

Chapter Thirty

Arnold boarded the train, unsure of where he was going. He couldn't bear to head home, but he also had nowhere to go. He went by instinct, hopping on the first train he saw, heading toward the Loop. He closed his eyes, listening to the name of each station. He didn't want to see any spirits, couldn't bear to see any part of the world he needed to deny. He'd get an appointment to up his meds on Monday, and that was that.

When the train pulled into Fullerton, he stood without thinking, hurrying across the concrete platform to board the Red Line. The DePaul stadium was below, a handful of baseball players running around in their uniforms. Arnold tried not to look, keeping his eyes on the floor as he found a seat. He picked one at random, terrified he'd draw the seat-preference grass again. With his eyes shut, he cast around him in his mind, but thankfully, he didn't sense anything. Had breaking up with Helen banished them, waking him from whatever beautiful dream he'd stumbled into?

Of course, Nüste could be right — he'd shut his third eye. But if that's what it took to have a normal life, he'd do it. This wasn't real. It *couldn't* be real. He cracked his eyes open, grateful there was nothing there to see. He glanced at his shoulder, and thankfully, even the spinning black orb was gone. Part of him was worried he really had left it at Helen's, but he had to let that go. He'd done the right thing, freeing Helen of whatever was wrong with him. Now, she'd have a chance to forget him before he wormed his way deeper into her life.

Without another dimension to worry about, it was nice to look out the window. He thought he saw something massive floating among the clouds, but he ignored it, focusing on the buildings instead. The train rolled ever northward, passing Uptown and Little Vietnam. He watched as people wandered about below, some with grocery baskets, others heading into restaurants. How nice it must feel to be normal! For a moment, part of him had been grateful to be weird, happy to see the little mysteries of life. And Helen... She'd fallen for the real him, hadn't she? Even if he was the same person who'd ruined everything, he was the one she'd wanted for that brief, incredible moment.

He shook his head, looking east as the lake finally appeared, glimpses of perfect blue flashing between the giant sixties condos in Edgewater. He'd had a friend in middle school who'd lived in one of those. Up on the twenty-fifth floor, when he woke up after their sleepovers, all he could see was blue, the waves crashing in from infinity as the sun rose.

Finally, passing Loyola, he decided to get off. He suddenly needed to be by the water, to stare into the distance and forget about all his problems back on land.

He walked north, passing by the old stone buildings of the university. He wanted to reach the dock, where he and Dad used to fish when he was younger. They'd gone every Saturday in summer, his dad teaching him how to tie the lines. Couldn't he have just stayed small like that? He hated the age he'd entered into, this era when everyone looked at him like he was broken, useless.

He cut over to the beach on Lunt, passing by the old three-flats, their stone facades looking like they'd been built much longer than a century ago. Maybe it was the weather, the winter wind coming off the lake to hammer them season after season. One even had gargoyles on the roof, with nothing left of their expression but a row of teeth, forever growling at the neighbors as they passed.

Passing the little fence at the end of the block, he crossed onto the sand, the sound of the waves rushing up to greet him. He kept his shoes on, clomping over to where the tide had run out and the sand was firm enough to hold his weight. He kept his eyes on the horizon, watching as the lakebed disappeared beneath the crystalline water. There were a few sailboats but nothing else, the vanishing point interrupted only by the pumping stations in the distance, pulling water from the lake into the city.

He *did* feel better, calmer. Being out here felt like its own kind of dream, like finding the parts of himself that he'd forgotten. If only he had a boat. He could sail away right now, disappearing before he ruined anything else. He'd ride through the Mackinac Straits and up the St. Lawrence Seaway, never to be heard from again. But no, he only had this life. The miserable, broken life he was already barely hanging on to.

He walked out on the concrete pier, the rusted metal gunwale running two hundred feet into the waves. When he got to the end, he sat, looking down into the water, his legs dangling off the edge. Once he could stop, once he was still, all his feelings came running after him. He finally allowed himself to cry, the numbness washing away as his tears fell into the waves, disappearing into the darkness of the lake. How many tears would it take to turn the water salty? An impossibility, not unlike his attempt to change his life.

"I wish I was different," he whispered, his throat tight from crying. "I wish I wasn't such a mess. I wish I was lovable. I wish…"

He closed his eyes, pushing out his tears, the twin rivers on his face widening to a flood. He couldn't say the last part, couldn't admit how badly he wished he wasn't broken or how much he loved Helen, how deeply he wanted to be good enough for her. But already, he'd messed everything up. He'd nearly thrown away his second chance, and he wasn't going to get a third.

But what was it he was even trying to salvage? Was this really a life? Even if he finished school, graduating wouldn't magically fill the holes in his soul, wouldn't replace whatever it was his heart was missing. He didn't have what everyone else did, the thing that allowed them to get up every day, to look in the mirror without disgust. He—

Child?

Arnold wiped his eyes, looking for the voice. He'd thought there weren't any spirits here. He'd *thought* he'd finally shut them out, that they would finally leave him be. It wasn't a gift to see these things, it was a curse. A curse that had nearly destroyed him. He'd tried to do something good with his visions, had tried to help Helen. But in the end, he would only drag her down with him. Letting her go was the only thing to do.

He took a deep breath, trying to clear his mind. He looked back down into the water. He was just hearing things. It wasn't real, it—

He saw a spirit in the lake, two giant eyes staring up at him. In the darkness of the water, he could just make it out. It was like a giant blanket on the lakebed, a blob of blue somehow different from the water flowing all around it. Actually, it was sort of like the creatures Fujimoto releases in *Ponyo*, the pillars of water sent out to find his daughter.

"Are you real?" Arnold whispered. His voice sounded far away, like it wasn't his own. Should he even bother asking anymore? Would he know the truth if he saw it?

As real as you, the spirit thought.

"That isn't saying much."

The spirit seemed to laugh, the water rippling beneath Arnold's feet. It foamed against the pier, bubbles bunching up until they disappeared, broken up by the next set of waves. He'd heard somewhere that waves always came in sevens, the tallest one always coming first.

I thought men had forgotten to speak to the sea.

The sea? In Lake Michigan? Of course, he'd realized long ago that the differences between things weren't the same for people and spirits. Maybe all water was the same, or maybe this thing was in more than one place.

"Are you…the spirit of the sea?"

No. I'm old, but not old enough for that. I've only seen her once. She stays much deeper than I do, undisturbed by human life. I'm a spirit of wishes, I suppose.

"You grant wishes?"

If only, the spirit thought. It seemed to sigh, as if it had its own wishes it had been forced to abandon piling up beneath the sand. *I'm not the spirit of the wish but of the wishing, the result of humans speaking to the water, hoping for a different life. I...have no way of knowing if they come true. Not many have returned to thank or curse me. After all these years, you're the first who's ever met my eyes.*

"So, what's the point? Why bother wishing at all?"

The spirit hummed, not denying the question. Maybe it was a pointless one, but he felt he had to ask it, felt he *deserved* an answer. After all, why show him all these spirits if it meant nothing? Even if it was all made up by his subconscious, a figment of his broken imagination, it had to mean *something*, didn't it?

The purpose of a wish, child, is the wishing. Even if it doesn't come true, there's a part of you that thinks you deserve to dream, to seek a better life. Part of you that knows something else is possible, even if it's just outside your reach. This is a thing of humans, of souls and yearning. You wish, and so you dream. You dream, and so you act. You act, and so you change. Is there anything in the world more powerful than that?

"I wish I was good enough for Helen," he whispered, finally forcing himself to say it. If what the spirit said was true, then there was no taking it back. Even if it didn't come true, there was a part of him wishing it was possible. A part of him that wouldn't be able to live with himself if he didn't try to make it so. Maybe it wasn't even about Helen specifically — even if he'd never met anyone so wonderful. But that was the point of love, wasn't it? It showed you the holes in your heart you hadn't healed, the doors you hadn't opened, making you want to walk through them and out into the light. Love was a mirror *and* a window, forcing you to see yourself before you leapt to the other side.

A good wish, the spirit said. It lingered for a moment, its giant eyes on him. It blinked slowly, as if savoring his dream. *I hope it comes true.*

Then, the spirit disappeared, receding into the waves until there was nothing left but the setting sun and the lapping of the water against the pier.

Arnold got up, looking out at the water one last time before he started walking toward land. He wouldn't go back to Helen, but he wouldn't give up either. He refused to weigh her down with his illness, but he would find a way to get his life on track, find a way to prove that he was whole. Even if that meant going back to the hospital, even if it meant proving these spirits were a delusion, he would do it. Whatever it took, he wanted to be whole again.

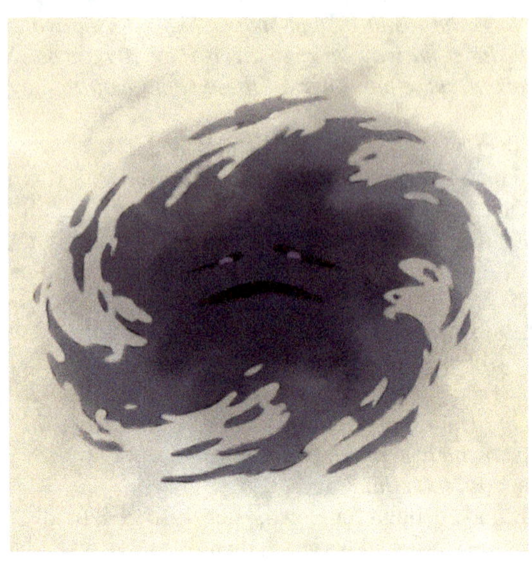

Chapter Thirty-one

Helen sat in the bakery for a long time. She stared at a single point on the wall, unmoving as her mind crowded with thoughts. They felt like a weight hanging above her, pressing down as they squeezed out her tears. An entire lifetime of regret seemed to bear down at her all at once. She thought of Gran, of all the years they'd wasted not being together. She thought of Arnold, and the love she'd scared away. She thought of everyone in Boston, an entire circle of friends she'd left behind to start this place. She tried not to think of her dad, but he was there too, and she was no longer strong enough to keep him out.

She looked down at the notebook, at Arnold's drawings. She'd flipped through them one by one, hoping she could find the thread that had made him leave her. Instead, she'd found something *wonderful*. They were beautiful, fascinating even. It made her mourn the art career he'd left behind, the videos she'd watched so many times. And then, at the end, she'd found herself, an undeserving idol.

Suddenly, there was a taste on her tongue, a bitter taste. But as it rippled through each taste bud, she found its flavor all too familiar. It tasted like the funeral home where they'd had Dad's memorial, the first time she'd seen Gran in ages at that point. It was strangely herbal, like an old medicine. This flavor had something to tell you, sins it wanted you to answer for. *If you could only learn its lesson*, it seemed to say, *then maybe you'd stop repeating all the same mistakes.*

"Self-loathing," she whispered, finally able to name it.

Could you bake something like that? Its flavors, at least, were all too common. It had cilantro and anise, garlic and brown sugar. They were all flavors she was more than fond of on their own, but when they were rolled together, they only had one thing to say — you *deserve* this. She imagined dyeing them with squid ink, her bakery churning out cupcakes full of darkness, reminding each Chicagoan of the terrible things they'd done.

The sun finally started setting, cutting through the buildings past the train station and into the bakery. Like a lance made of light, it pierced the darkness, making her blink as the room turned to gold. She looked around, shuddering as she realized how long she'd been sitting there. The flavor melted off her tongue, taking with it every horrible thing she'd been remembering. It was almost like something had been pressing on her mind, something...*alive*. She glanced up at the attic. What if Arnold really *was* seeing spirits? What if he was out there alone, feeling as horrible as she'd just felt?

She stood, looking toward the train as if he'd still be there, as if an hour hadn't slipped away with her staring into space. Part of her was offended. After all, *he'd* just broken up with *her*. But beyond the hurt, she could sense his pain — had seemingly just literally *tasted* it on her tongue — and that well of empathy smothered her hurt, covering it in love until it didn't feel so huge. More than that, though, even *if* none of this was real, she felt aligned with him. He was seeing things, and she was *tasting* things. Was that really so different? Should they be alone in this, or should they come together in their self-deception?

She was horrified by the dark turn her mind had taken, poised to turn her bakery into a factory for hatred. But what if she did something different? What if she took this feeling and baked its *opposite*? It felt like the kind of thing she'd been looking for all along. She'd always wanted to bake *good* feelings for her customers — hope, joy, *fun*. That was basically the entire point of baking. But what if she found something even more powerful? What if she could bake a kind of medicine, taking everyone's worst feelings and baking them a cure?

She moved on instinct, jumping behind the counter and into the kitchen. She banged around, slamming down bowls and whisks before she could lose her momentum. Did flavors even have opposites? Suddenly, she felt as if they might, as if she'd unlocked some secret theory of flavor, the hidden quarks making all her baked goods spin. Instead of cilantro, she used cardamom. Instead of anise, she used cherry. She started mixing it all into cookies, feeling like Gran was at her side, ready to do battle with the demons who whispered that she should hate herself.

Before she knew it, they were in the oven, the beautiful smell pouring through the vents and banishing what was left of the gloom spinning all around her. She leaned against the counter and laughed, her therapist's suggestion suddenly coming back to her. Maybe she knew how to practice self-compassion after all.

———

Nüste was in a panic. Below, he could sense the spirit of self-loathing growing bigger. It pulsed like a black hole, threatening to suck all the light of the world inside it. Even worse, he could sense Helen near it, her soul fluttering at the edge of the whirlpool. He could sense the void in her as well, its echo reaching for the darkness. After all, there had to be an anchor inside a human already for a pure emotion to enter; everyone knew that.

Unfortunately, for his chances of escape, this was an ominous sign — and a regrettably human one. Why was it that only humans could turn on themselves, driving their violence inward? There was power in humans, true — there was a reason he was so often attracted to them as a spirit of new beginnings — but this was proof of how dangerous they were too. If only he'd been drawn somewhere else this time.

Curse you, Arnold! he shouted to no one, pacing around the attic. Nüste *had* recruited the boy, but he refused to blame himself. It was humans who made the world this way. After all, there was a reason only an unstable youth like Arnold would let his third eye open in the first place. Everyone else was too busy destroying things with capitalism, bustling about their meaningless jobs while ignoring everything else. If they were willing to destroy the planet for gain, then what made him think they'd spare the spirit world?

Helen isn't like that, he thought, the sentiment coming unbidden. And she wasn't. She was something different in the human soup of indifference. Humans couldn't all be bad — or else spirits would be too. Just look at all the things humans had created. They even had enough technology to solve climate change; they were simply refusing to look at themselves in the mirror and change. But not Helen. She was trying, wasn't she? Was that why he'd been brought to her? He still didn't know what her new beginning was — couldn't even get her to look inside the attic — but maybe it was something wonderful, something world-changing.

He had to try again. He looked up at the ceiling, spotting a few ripples of leftover emotion. He started climbing the boxes. Maybe if he could knock down a bit of something else, it would shake Helen free of Arnold's curse. It sounded foolish, but he had to try. He suddenly had the distinct feeling that if he failed to save Helen now, he wouldn't simply be imprisoned here forever. He'd be snuffed out, his spiritual energy dissipating as any hope of her new beginning vanished. What would happen then? He'd never died before, every new beginning he'd been drawn to eventually fulfilled. He—

Can't think about that now. The girl needs you!

He climbed with everything he had, willing his increasingly corporeal form up the cardboard mountain on the side of the attic. Normally, he could will a bit of energy off the ceiling from where he was, but it was too distant, too thin to do so without getting closer. He gritted his nonexistent teeth, scrambling up with all his might. He had to get to her, had to—

That smell.

He stopped, something from the kitchen below finally catching his awareness. It was a new bake, a *wonderful* bake. Somehow, it had a light emanating from it, its spiritual signatures rotating on an opposite axis from the self-loathing, pushing it back on a subatomic level. It was *incredible*. Nüste flopped down on the boxes, weeping from every inch of his mushroom shell. *Helen, you brave, beautiful girl.*

——

The moment Helen took the cookies out of the oven, she knew they were perfect. The smell alone seemed to latch around her mind, filling her with hope. This was a powerful flavor. She liked to think about how bears could smell things miles away, a single particle enough to fill their nose with information.

She pried one off the tray with a spatula, dropping it onto a plate. She stared at it, drumming her fingers. It would be too hot to eat, but how could she wait with a discovery like this? She leaned over, blowing on it with all her might. She'd always been terrible at waiting for cookies, earning enough burns for Gran to start calling her "fire mouth." Fortunately, like the ends of her fingers in cooking school, a lifetime of blisters and calluses had earned her the right to eat cookies before anyone else.

She bit off one end, closing her eyes as an avalanche of memories hit her. Like a casting of molten metal, it wormed its way into her mind, seeking out the parts of her she thought she'd hidden. The memories came to her anyway, bursting open every door she'd locked from her childhood. This time, though, the flavor of self-compassion wrapped around them in a haze of light, making her feel warm and weightless, like floating in a bathtub.

"I'm scared," she said. Or *did* she say it? A voice rang out clearly in her mind — her voice — but she was younger, so much younger. How old was she then? Six? Seven? She'd been on the phone with Mom.

Somehow, Dad had won custody the year before, his living situation with Gran — and her house in the city — no doubt part of the equation. Mom was an immigrant, too new to English to sway the judge. But Dad had started using again, something her young brain couldn't comprehend. The stress of the divorce, problems at work, who knew? He was such a good dad, though, wasn't he? Good memories danced at the edges of the dark ones, reminding her of who he'd really been. He *wasn't* his addiction, but how was she supposed to understand all that in kindergarten? How was she supposed to keep his secrets from Mom on their weekly calls, the broken glass in the kitchen only just picked up that morning.

Gran's face floated up to her, younger, the day at the courthouse when Mom finally won custody back. The tears in Gran's eyes when she hugged Helen goodbye.

"I'm sorry," she said, crying into Gran's sweater. "I'm sorry."

"No, child, no. No sorry. No, no."

Where was Dad in that memory? Had he made it to court after failing the drug test? Had he been home at all those last few weeks? She heard again the terrible words she'd whispered to Mom on the phone all those months before.

"I'm scared."

Why did she have to say that? She'd set off the second custody battle, caused

Dad's downward spiral. The self-loathing fought against the flavor of the cookie, its needles of anger and blame poking at the edges of the light. Somehow, though, the flavor held, the light shuttling her along like a roller coaster, through the darkness toward the next memory. Unfortunately, she knew what it would be, the one memory she never wanted to think about, the worst one of them all.

More tears, a casket, some random funeral home in Elgin. She was only nine, but so many people had come up to talk to her.

"We loved your dad," they'd say. "I'm sorry for your loss."

She wanted to scream. She didn't know these people. How could they have any idea? She'd been separated from Gran by an ocean of strangers, unable to reach her across the stuffy funeral parlor. All she'd wanted was to apologize, to tell Gran how sorry she was, to beg her to let her come and spend the summers with her in the city. How many more years until Mom would let her do just that? Four? Five?

"It's all my fault," she whispered, standing at the casket's edge. Closed but ominous, the wood was much too shiny for what it held. The funeral home director had instructed her to write a letter, which they had slipped into a hole at the casket's base like a mailbox for the dead. She hadn't known what to write. *I'm sorry*, she'd finally scrawled on it, only just having started cursive. *I love you.*

"It's not your fault," a voice said, breaking through the memory. It was a voice made of light, though it sounded familiar. Was it hers? It was her adult self, reaching for her inner child, desperate to tear her away from all that suffering. "It's not your fault," the voice repeated. She suddenly saw herself in her memory, reaching out to hug that inner child, so lost and confused. Helen hugged herself, holding on for dear life as the memories tugged at her. "It's not your fault."

Helen opened her eyes, blinking through the tears to look at the cafe full of light, the sunset giving up its final rays. She felt like the light was passing through her, banishing the shadows she'd been carrying so long. How could she have ever blamed herself?

"Speak how you would speak to a friend," she said, laughing through the tears at how obvious her therapist's advice felt now. You would *never* tell a nine-year-old her father's death was her fault. *Because it wasn't.* It wasn't Dad's fault, either. Life was a beautiful, chaotic, hard, terrible, lovely thing. Sometimes you lost the things you love. Sometimes *you* were the thing that ended up lost.

She took a deep breath, laughing for no reason at all. The entire house seemed lighter, as if a weight had been taken off the roof, the wood and brick no longer groaning from the effort of holding all that heartache. She looked up toward the attic, a room she'd avoided for far too long. She grabbed another cookie, shoving it in her mouth like it was armor as she headed for the stairs.

Chapter Thirty-two

Helen moved quickly through the house, flipping on lights as she went, the sun quickly disappearing. But for the first time, heading to the attic didn't feel like entering some evil, lightless tunnel. This time, she was the intrepid explorer, climbing a mountain in search of hidden treasure. Maybe it was just the effect of the cookies, but she simply couldn't see what the big deal was anymore.

"Just an attic," she said to herself, her hand finally on the doorknob to the final set of stairs.

The memories of fearing this place were still there, but they were hazier somehow, like remembering the first day of school on the day you graduate. Everything had become familiar, like furniture you no longer bumped into in the dark.

"I can do this."

She wrenched open the door, sprinting up the steps to where the only light was turned on by pulling a string. Maybe running proved she was a *teensy* bit afraid, but only of the dark! She wasn't a total fool.

For an attic, it actually wasn't that bad. It had two large windows showing the street below, and despite all her neglect, it wasn't full of spiders or anything. She probably should have used it as an office, a place to read in the summer when the light poured in. She was—

There were *teacups* on the ground. Sitting on saucers, they were scattered throughout the attic.

"Creepy…" she said, feeling a shiver go up her spine.

Still, she didn't run. Something about it was too innocent to be terrifying.

Even if the attic was haunted, a poltergeist that liked to play tea couldn't be all bad, right? After all, this *was* a bakery. It also reminded her of Arnold seeing spirits. Could it be that he really hadn't made it up? Her first instinct had been to believe him. How else could she explain the flavors she kept tasting?

"I'm...uh...sorry I haven't been up here in a while," she announced to the room. Part of her wondered again if it could be Gran, though she honestly doubted the woman could ever be a ghost. Helen had held her hand as she died, and she'd been utterly at peace, simply nodding off under the weight of the hospice drugs. Besides, Gran wasn't the type to hold on to things. Perhaps it was part of coming to Chicago as an immigrant, but the woman didn't *do* unfinished business.

"Whoever you are," she whispered, "I promise I'll try to visit more."

Hopefully that would be enough. Spirits were about intention, weren't they? You simply had to say the right words and mean them. Then again, if she was planning on coming up here more often, she'd have to actually go through the boxes piled all around her. Today, though, there was only one she needed to open.

Like a magnet on her mind, it seemed to call to her. Off to the right and jammed between two others, the box was old, the crumpled cardboard emblazoned with the name of some long-folded moving company from the nineties. On the side, in permanent market, she'd scrawled a single word — *DAD*.

It took her a few minutes to extricate it, a bit of Jenga she very nearly failed at. After almost knocking over an antique clock, she finally had Dad's things all on their own, dragging them to the center of the room. She sat on the floor, taking a deep breath as she pulled open the top, the cardboard wedged together instead of taped.

It didn't take long before she was crying again. The first thing she found was his White Sox jersey, the old acrylic stitched with the name *Fisk* across the back. She held it against her face, remembering all the times they'd ridden the train back from the games, her tiny frame asleep against his on the way home. It didn't smell like him anymore, but it seemed to summon him all the same.

The rest of the box was a delightful jumble of odds and ends, things Gran had apparently been collecting for him all the way back to high school. There were a bunch of yearbooks — she hadn't even realized he'd gone to Amundsen — trophies and ribbons, greeting cards. There was even a wooden thing he must have whittled as a Boy Scout, though what it was supposed to be was beyond her.

Helen took each item out in turn, like a miner sifting through a pile of gems. Soon, she had a little stack next to her, a jumble of beauty with no particular organizing principle. And there, at the bottom, was the most precious thing of all, something she never would have dreamed of finding — an envelope with her name on it. Written in what must have been Dad's blocky script, the *H* in *Helen* was huge compared to the other letters. She picked it up, cradling it against her chest.

What could this be? When they were separated, she'd hardly known how to write herself. And in the short, terrible years between then and when he died, he'd never once sent her a letter. They had *some* visitation rights, and she remembered those trips well enough. But they'd never talked about what she did, never aired any sentiment other than hugging hello and goodbye — and trying to win prizes at the arcade or whatever else they ended up doing with the friend of the court looming over his shoulder. She sucked in a deep breath — her face full of tears and snot — and opened the letter.

> Dear Helen,
> I don't know if I'll give this to you, but I'm in rehab and we're writing letters. Maybe Gran can do it when you're older. I wanted to say I'm sorry. I let you down. You shouldn't have to see the things you saw, and I'm glad you're safe with your mother now. Gran and I miss you, but that's why I'm trying to get better. You kept saying you were sorry at court, but this isn't your fault. Sometimes life is hard, but there's always hope for something better. Having a wonderful daughter like you keeps me grateful in here. I still remember bringing you home from the hospital. How beautiful you were, all your tiny fingers and toes. You're my favorite girl in the whole world. I hope I'll see you soon.
>
> Love,
> Dad

She shut her eyes, a fresh river of tears wetting her cheeks. She quickly put the letter back, afraid she'd get it wet. She shook as she sobbed, but immediately, she felt so much *lighter*, an impossible weight lifting from her shoulders. Even with her strange cookie-fueled breakthrough downstairs — and finding the strength to finally forgive herself — it felt impossibly freeing to see that he'd forgiven her too.

She wiped her eyes, laughing as she sniffled. To think she'd left this up here so long! When had he written this? She picked up the letter to look for a date, hoping she—

Good job, kid, a voice said behind her.

Helen whipped around, ready to bolt, when she came face to face with a little mushroom. Or a mushroom...*man*? It was standing on a nearby box exuding...happiness. Could mushrooms be happy? It was... *Wait. It was one of Arnold's drawings.*

I was wondering when you'd finally come up here, the mushroom said in her mind. *Seems Arnold wasn't a total loser after all.*

"You're...?"

The teacups suddenly made sense, her fear dissipating. It was like finding a squirrel in the woods when you expected wolves. The warmth this thing exuded, the way it talked to her... She didn't *feel* in danger.

I'm just leaving, the spirit answered, chuckling. *But the name's Nüste. Seems my work here is done. I'm proud of you, though. Enjoy that new beginning, eh?*

With that, the little mushroom disintegrated before her eyes, turning into light, a thousand little orbs filling the attic like the sun. And then, something *shifted*, the dancing lights drifting off, passing through the walls as they disappeared. Helen sat, staring up at the ceiling. *Arnold.* The mushroom man had mentioned him by name. She remembered then the way he'd hesitated, looking up at the attic when he'd assured her there were no spirits in the house.

So, it *was* real. Arnold was real, her baking was real, *she* was real. More importantly, it seemed there was a way to save what they had, the beautiful, broken little bird of a romance she'd feared had flown away forever. It was another bit of magic, an incredible thing she couldn't explain — but those were seemingly everywhere these days. The cookies, finding Dad's letter, it felt like she'd opened a perpendicularity, all the world's dimensions merging into one.

Or she'd well and truly lost it. Still, she felt happier, more whole than she had in years. More importantly, something *had* changed in the attic. The place felt as light and airy as she did. Her new beginning… She got up, packing up Dad's box. The letter, however, she tucked into her pocket. It would be coming with her. Maybe she'd even frame it in the bakery. But first, there was something she had to do.

Chapter Thirty-three

Arnold rode the train to school, his eyes bleary. Still, he felt…normal? Or normal enough, anyway. He'd gotten home from the beach to find a bag of cookies from Lois hanging on his door. He ate them by the kitchen sink, letting the familiar sounds of his apartment lull him into submission. Sleep hadn't come easily, but he'd been grateful to be in the quiet of his place, staring at the moldy ceiling, not a spirit in sight. *Normal.* He could be normal.

Maybe it was just being tired, but so far that morning, he hadn't seen a single strange thing. It was an oddly hopeful feeling. At least compared to the raging self-loathing he'd felt the day before. Even if he was just getting back into his routine, it felt like he was taking action, moving himself in the right direction again. Not sleeping would hardly help him boost his grades, but it was only a temporary measure. After school, he had an appointment at the clinic, and he would sort all this out.

When he got off the train and went to his bus stop, he didn't even stop to look at the sky. Why jinx it? Best-case scenario, the giant silver ring wasn't there, and he could center himself with a view of the clouds. But worst-case scenario… He started pacing, looking at the transit app. Where was that bus anyway? By the time it came, he could— *No.* He refused to run away from this. With his delusional thinking, every inch he gave up was a thousand miles. He took a deep breath, looking at the sky. There…was *nothing* there.

His eyes flicked around the intersection. The train station, the Filipino bakery, the bar with the jukebox. Every part of Chicago was as it had always been, sitting peacefully beneath a bright blue sky, a herd of puffy clouds making their way out to pasture. By all accounts — his own problems notwithstanding — it was a lovely spring day. He had nothing to fear.

By the time he reached the school, he was feeling almost *confident*. Or whatever normal people meant by confidence. He at least felt capable, looking into the cemetery with only a tiny bit of fear. Thankfully, he saw nothing there either. The graves, while a bit macabre in their own way, were no different than the baseball fields to his right. Just ground and grass, no terror of the spirit realm coming to haunt him. No ghost, no—

"Helen?" he asked, stopping in the middle of the sidewalk. She was sitting on a bench by the baseball field, a pink box in her hands. Or was she? Had he traded all his other delusions for just this one, the specter of her beauty the only thing left clinging to his mind?

"Hey," she said, waving as she stood. "Sorry to surprise you here, I… Are you okay?"

He looked behind him, glancing at the cemetery once more, but there was still nothing there. Was she real, then? It was terrifying to not be able to trust yourself, to wonder. But she must be real, she had to be.

"I'm fine, sorry. You surprised me is all. I… Are you starting school here?"

"No, silly. I was looking for you."

Had she come to yell at him for breaking up with her? If anything, it had gone *too* smoothly the night before, her understanding even more painful than the anger he'd expected. He braced himself. He deserved whatever curses she had for him. Of course, most people didn't use pink boxes to attack their exes. Or their *friends*? They did only go on two dates, but he still felt awful for leading her on.

"Sorry if it's too soon," she said, eyeing his chest where he'd folded his arms. Remembering his lecture on body language in a therapeutic setting, he opened them, trying to keep his hands still at his sides.

"No, it's okay. Sorry. You…aren't here to yell at me, are you?"

Thankfully, she laughed. "No. I'm here to… Well, I guess do whatever the opposite of yelling is? I don't know how, but you *did* something to me, *changed* me. Being around you helped me heal something I've spent a long time avoiding, and I guess I just wanted to return the favor." She bit her lip, no doubt seeing his confusion. "Sorry, I'm talking in circles. Does the name…*Nüste* mean anything to you?"

Nüste… He looked over his shoulder again, the whole world seeming to rock around him. He didn't know what to think. He'd never mentioned that name to anyone. Hadn't written down or put it in a search engine. But if this was real. If she was real…

"How…?" was all he managed to say, no other words coming out, his mouth suddenly dry.

"We met last night. In the attic. I don't think you're as unstable as you think, Arnold. In fact, I think you're wonderful. You came to the bakery to help me, didn't you?"

"I…" Should he deny it? Wasn't it creepy? He didn't want her to feel like the spirits had sent him to spy on her. Or wait… Was he taking them seriously again? Was he… "Yes. I mean, wow."

"I know," she said, the smile never leaving her lips. "After we talked, I was feeling awful, and I baked a cookie, and… I should come clean too. I bake feelings. It sounds silly, I know, but it's true. After everything I've seen, I can't deny it anymore. And then hearing about what you saw… I guess I'm open to a lot more than I used to be." She took a breath. "How about I just show you?"

She opened her box, revealing a giant stack of cookies. Cut into hearts, they had two parts, one with pink frosting and the other plain. On the plain side, they looked like shortbread with pieces of cherries folded into the dough. He thought of all the other things she'd baked for him, their uncanny ability to bring up memories. Was that all real too? He felt unmoored again, but this time, it wasn't a bad feeling. It was the feeling of floating, of being *free*.

She smiled, nodding for him to take one. He held it in his hand, the cookie still holding a lingering warmth from the oven. He took a bite from the plain half, a memory coming to him. But it wasn't an old memory. Strangely, it was everything he'd experienced the past few weeks, played back for him. And within the storm of images, he kept seeing Helen, her bright eyes, her wide smile.

Was she looking at *him* in those memories? Was that the face she made when he was near her? Such *happiness*, a feeling he'd never imagined inspiring in someone else.

He *had* helped her after all.

Whatever happened next, he finally felt a weight lift from his shoulders he hadn't realized he'd been carrying. He hadn't ruined her life, and he hadn't ruined his either. In fact, he'd never ruined anything. What happened at art school wasn't his fault, and it wasn't his animation's fault either. He'd just been too hard on himself, too terrified of who he might become. How had he never realized that before? Now, he couldn't wait to find out what his future held, especially if it had Helen in it.

He started crying before he realized it, but suddenly, Helen was there, her arms tight around him. He cried into her shoulder, sobbing as he was freed from every burden he'd accumulated over the years, every wound of adulthood that had turned into a scar deep within his heart.

"It's alright," she whispered, squeezing him tighter, the pink box pressed against his back. "It's gonna be alright."

Finally, he caught his breath, wiping his eyes as they separated. "And…Nüste?"

"He left," she said, looking up at the sky. He followed her eyes, finding the silver ring back where it belonged. "He told me to enjoy my new beginning."

"And did you get one? Did you…find what you were looking for?"

"I think so," she said, smiling. "But there's something else I want too. Why don't you eat the pink half?"

He glanced down at the cookie, only then realizing he hadn't eaten any of the icing. Something had drawn him to the plain part first.

"What's in the pink part?"

"Well, it isn't just *one* kind of cookie. The plain part is 'self-compassion.' But before you came over yesterday, I'd been working on something else. A cookie…for kissing."

He laughed, looking at the cookie in his hand.

"Hey!" she said. "Don't laugh, it's—"

He kissed her, the cookie clutched tightly in his hand. She melted into him, kissing him back. He kept his eyes closed, never wanting the dream to end. But even without seeing it, he could feel the world bubbling up around him, could sense the pink butterflies filling the air. Finally, they separated, and she held his gaze, her eyes shining.

"See?" she said, laughing. "This *is* going to be fun."

THE END